Love is
a time of enchantment:
in it all days are fair and all fields
green. Youth is blest by it,
old age made benign:
the eyes of love see
roses blooming in December,
and sunshine through rain. Verily
is the time of true-love
a time of enchantment — and
Oh! how eager is woman
to be bewitched!

NURSE ELSA

When Nurse Elsa Hoyt signed on at Port Haven Hospital, she discovered that the chief of staff was her stepfather, who had broken her mother's heart. She was on the point of resigning when her stepfather begged her to stay, but suggested she not admit she knew him. To further complicate matters, Elsa was confronted by the hostility of one young doctor, the inexplicable friendship of another medico, and the interest of a nurse with whom she had little in common.

Books by Jeanne Bowman
in the Ulverscroft Large Print Series:

NEIGHBORHOOD NURSE
GIRL EXECUTIVE

JEANNE BOWMAN

NURSE ELSA

Complete and Unabridged

ULVERSCROFT
Leicester

First published in the
United States of America
under the title 'Nurse À La Mode'

First Large Print Edition
published April 1994

British Library CIP Data

Bowman, Jeanne
    Nurse Elsa.—Large print ed.—
    Ulverscroft large print series: romance
    I. Title
    813.52 [F]

    ISBN 0–7089–3054–9

Published by
F. A. Thorpe (Publishing) Ltd.
Anstey, Leicestershire

Set by Words & Graphics Ltd.
Anstey, Leicestershire
Printed and bound in Great Britain by
T. J. Press (Padstow) Ltd., Padstow, Cornwall

This book is printed on acid-free paper

1

"THERE is one field cybernetics won't control: the nursing profession!"

Elsa Hoyt, R.N., heard the sharp incisive voice sound from the patio outside, and laughter touched the blue of her eyes, even as she eased her patient into a lounging chair.

Mrs. Gardner looked up to reflect the smile. "It would take a patient a little too long to know which button to press to adjust an inanimate object for comfort, wouldn't it?" Then, warming to the subject, she pictured a long arm reaching out from a machine, prying open a reluctant mouth and inducing into it the right capsule; or changing the bandage on a suppurating area.

Elsa thought of many other services she doubted could be computerized, then glanced out above the patio to many roofs and, beyond, slim towers reaching to the sky. The roofs were the home base

1

of astronauts, the towers missile guides.

Man spends billions to explore and conquer space, she mused, while he himself and his relationship to his fellow man remains comparatively unknown.

The voice in the patio came again, irritated now. "How would I know? It's surrounded by military bases, isn't it? All right. Nurse marries, retires to home life; then comes a call. She qualifies by taking duty in the nearest hospital. Ah, but let her husband be recalled, or she divorced, or any number of circumstances occur, and she swings right back into the arm of the service where she originally trained.

"All I do know is this. Port Haven Hospital is so short of nurses I've seen the medicos fill in, in an emergency. Shame, too. Fine staff — "

"Nurse, *nurse!*" Mrs. Gardner tugged at Elsa's arm. "Is there something wrong?"

Wrong? Port Haven Hospital! She hadn't seen the edifice for years, or Port Haven. Yet the memories that welled up at the mention of its name!

"Wrong?" Elsa shook her head. "No; just wondering how such a place could cope. I mean it isn't like Chicago, where there is always the outside chance of the perfect nurse responding to a call. I assume Port Haven is relatively small."

Mrs. Gardner said it had been until others sought it as a recreation area because of its delightful climate, then, on being transferred, sold to permanent residents. And of course the port was active; cotton, bananas, rice, the usual for that climate.

She broke off suddenly to say, "My goodness, Dr. Crissman does have his dander or blood pressure up. You'd think he owned the hospital." And she quieted that Elsa might hear the next.

"All right, I did intern there. What? No, the man who used to own it sold out, took off north some place. Marital trouble, I understand. Still privately owned, but by a group."

And then she said Elsa must take a little rest. She doubted she'd slept on the plane coming down; too busy looking after her patient, who was herself tired.

Rest? Elsa went willingly to the lovely guest room to sink into a deep chair. 'The man who used to own it' had

3

been her stepfather. And there had been marital trouble: a separation, a divorce. She didn't know why herself. She'd been sent north to a private school. She did know her mother had never been the same afterward, refusing to allow Dr. Hoag's name to be mentioned in her hearing.

There had been a basic settlement of some sort, but no alimony, and her mother had gone back to nursing.

She had even returned to using the name Hoyt, not too dissimilar from Hoag.

'Well, no wonder she didn't object to my accompanying my patient south, if Dad sold out and moved away.' It would be fun to go down and visit old scenes. She doubted if any of her earlier school friends were still there, though they could be.

If I had a car, she mused, then sat up, alert. Why not buy one — a used one, naturally — then drive herself back north instead of flying back. Be fun to have. Save time wasted waiting for cabs. And she had a vacation due her.

She'd slip out after dinner. Used

4

car lots were always open. Nor would the Gardners mind. She'd delivered Tom's mother in good condition after hospitalization following a tragic crash on Michigan Boulevard. Tom Gardner had said she'd even healed his mother's memories. Maybe alleviated them, she thought.

He said more that evening when she drove in with her purchase. A wonderful idea. But when she confessed what had triggered it, Dr. Crissman spoke up. She had signed off in Chicago for an indefinite time, hadn't she? Well, why not take a part-time vacation at Port Haven? Even a stand-by nurse would be a boon she owed her profession. Was there any reason she couldn't? Any commitments? Family responsibilities?

She had given a slight shake of her head. Her mother, a dean in a nurses' training school, was too busy to miss her. She might even be glad of a guest room instead of having a daughter under her feet in her off hours.

Elsa wasn't given time to weigh the pros and cons. At the shake of her head, Dr. Crissman was at the telephone

5

calling Port Haven Hospital, talking to the superintendent of nurses, telling her of one Elsa Hoyt, down from Chicago, whom he highly recommended.

Yes, she'd report in tomorrow. On a stand-by basis, it was to be understood.

Now, twelve hours later, Elsa faced the highway ahead, white, blinding white. She had forgotten how one's eyes recoiled from the Gulf-bleached sands and sun. Automatically she reached for the glove compartment, then withdrew her hand. She had also forgotten dark glasses.

How had she gotten herself into this?

A car slued close from the rear, accelerated and shot around.

All right, nurse; what would you tell a patient faced with fifty miles of this ahead? I'd say if you can't keep your eyes on it, keep your mind alert.

She wasted a moment looking out in wonderment at the change in the landscape. What had been lagoons or bog land in her childhood was now artistically diked waterways with equally artistic homes lining them.

The blinding glare struck again, and with it a memory. She and some tall, lanky schoolmate had headed for the west end of Port Haven to swim with a school group. His car had broken down en route. Another, heading east, had alerted the schoolmate's brother.

He'd also been tall, but somehow different, and with his coming had come easement. Dark glasses and a gentle scolding. She was a 'newcomer', and blue-eyed. Didn't she know it took the blues and the grays longer to adapt to glare than dark-eyed people?

She'd seen him again somewhere. A hazy memory, yet with it again came that sense of easement and comfort.

Ah, well, now to concentrate upon how she had started due south fifty miles instead of due north several hundred.

Like a tape recording synchronized with film came a rerun of the previous evening. The cocktail hour. A group of men in the patio, she with the patient in a room opening onto the cheerful spot.

Swiftly the miles sped under the car's wheels, and swiftly thoughts raced through Elsa's mind. Such phrases as 'How perfect; a paid-for vacation.' And 'Delightful here in the summer; always an

7

evening sea breeze.' 'A change from the wear and tear of Chicago.' 'Just imagine a dip in the Gulf, then stretching out in the warm sands, completely relaxed.'

A dip in the Gulf; an older memory stirred. She, who had come from the northwest originally, had been shocked when she had paddled into a low breaker. She had thought she'd stepped into a bathtub by mistake. The water was actually warm, but fun.

It would be again, yet — Elsa frowned. She was nearing the Causeway; the port city was a jagged line of roofs against the intense blue of the sky.

Probably all they had said was true. When she had asked about living quarters, there was a quick, 'Easy, this time of the year.' Then why was she taking such a disturbed attitude toward the venture?

Because — she was on the Causeway — it was not actually my decision. And if it were not, what was she doing there? Well, she was committed to a certain stretch at Port Haven. She would accept it was good; time later to come to some understanding with Bob Latoret. Writing was better than trying to talk to him.

8

He outtalks me, she thought, but did not question whether he spoke more quickly or more loudly, silencing her objections. Yet why should she marry this lab technician because he said they 'fused emotionally'? Once they were married, her metabolism could change and she would blow up sky high. That was her weakness, she was convinced: that she became so enraged. Her mind stopped short.

She had reached Port Haven, automatically driven due south and reached the wide boulevard spanning the island east and west, the avenue on which she had once lived. But the house was no longer there; instead, the entire area was taken over by high rise apartments.

At least it eased the shock of her first view of the hospital. When she was a child, say the time she was in for an appendectomy, the building had seemed made of adobe brick, with not too wide windows. This edifice was of steel and glass, even more modern in architecture than the Chicago hospital where she had trained.

This was good. This erased the

last memory-chain with the past. She wouldn't be treated as 'Dr. Hoag's girl; you know, his stepdaughter.' She wanted no special benefits'; merely, during such time as she spent on duty there, being treated as a nurse, period.

Car parked in the visitors' area, Elsa made her way to the main entrance. There were few cars and, when she entered, a lack of bustle she was accustomed to finding. Of course there were two other hospitals on the island, yet surely the clinic at this hour, regardless of the nurse shortage which would affect the hospital proper, should show more activity.

The girl at the reception desk looked at her with a completely dead-pan expression.

"Where will I find the superintendent of nurses?" Elsa asked. "I am Hoyt, from Chicago."

Ah, a spark of interest, and in a moment she was going down a long corridor filled with amber light and with artistic signs along the way indicating which suite could be found in what direction.

Elsa stopped at the proper door. Inside, at the main desk, sat a woman, chin propped by a cupped hand braced on the desk by her elbow. And even as Elsa looked the chin slipped off the hand.

The poor woman, thought Elsa. Bet she's been on twenty-four-hour duty. She is bushed. She herself slipped back, then cleared her throat and, feeling warning of her presence had been given, again appeared in the doorway.

"I am Hoyt of Chicago — " she began.

"Yes, yes, of course. Dr. Crissman called. I have been waiting for you."

I'll bet you have, thought Elsa; waiting when you should have been resting. Swiftly she herself pulled up a chair and methodically began giving the necessary information for Nurse Rawlings to document.

Even as Crissman had explained the dearth of nurses, so did Rawlings. Hoyt could understand Port Haven's geographical location would not be a center from which one called in an emergency. A stand-by nurse could be of great value, yet why just stand by?

"Perhaps," Elsa's blue eyes twinkled, You've been on constant duty long enough to concede a little rest is indicated." Then she explained that even the largest cities had their nurse-shortage problems, and that it was nearly as hard for a nurse to refuse duty as it was for a physician to refuse his services in an emergency.

The preliminaries over, there was a discussion of living quarters. Rawlings frowned, then said the only really adequate spot available was an apartment with a southeast exposure, Gulf breezes after a hot day. But one had to take a six-months lease.

Elsa felt an inward recoil. Six months! But she had intended to stay no more than a few weeks, a month at most.

"Here — " keys were thrust at her — "You look at it. Meanwhile, there are motels if you check in early enough. But do let the operator know where to reach you. You will?"

Bemused, Elsa moved out, keys dangling, and even as she turned from the superintendent's office noticed a figure coming along the corridor toward her. Doctor, her mind tabulated. Tall; light, almost white hair, in contrast to his tanned face. Must take his relaxation on the golf course. Or perhaps swimming.

She glanced up as they neared and found eyes the color of chestnuts staring at her. Brown eyes with that light hair? And the man was talking to himself. As she passed, she distinctly heard him say, "No, it can't be."

She looked back. He, too, had swerved to stare at her. Then both continued their original paths with an accelerated pace.

Had she ever seen him before? Surely she would have remembered.

And here came another. What a dreary color they wore here, a drab greenish gray. Probably the climate. This was an older man, and though he walked rapidly there was a slope to his shoulders which indicated, to her at least, that he carried a load too heavy to be borne.

An old man, yet not old. Those deep wrinkles on either side of his mouth looked rather as though someone had etched them with a scalpel. Hair, grey, very short. And now a glimpse of his eyes through heavily ground lenses.

"Ah — " he said.

"Oh, my word," breathed Elsa, and fled on. The man was Dr. Paul Hastings Hoag, her former stepfather. He hadn't 'sold out and moved north.' He was right there, in the hospital where she had just signed up to serve, on call.

Swiftly she spun along the corridor heading for the clinic reception room. Why hadn't she paid more attention to the staff register before she signed? And how could she peruse it without those behind the desk becoming interested?

She'd be adroit. She sank into a leather chair, made a bit of a fuss aligning the keys Nurse Rawlings had given her, looked up at the office staff, then turned her head.

She didn't have to search. There at the top of a list of names was his, as though emblazoned. Paul H. Hoag, Internal Medicine. Chief of staff.

Why had she let Crissman get her into this? Why hadn't she had sense enough to ask for a run-down on the medical men associated with Port Haven?

Above all, what was she going to do now?

There was only one thing to do, she reasoned. As soon as she had regained her poise, she would march right down to the superintendent's office and tell her she, Elsa, had changed her mind. And what would her answer be when she was asked what had caused such a quick change?

Given time, she might look at the apartment, at motels, then return and say she had found nothing acceptable. But could she? That would be a lie, and when had a lie ever been as effective as the truth?

Nor could she tell the truth: that she found it impossible to serve here, as her former stepfather was chief of staff. At that, would he have her even as a 'stand-by' nurse? And if he would, how could she ever explain to her mother?

A few patients entered, were handed their case histories at the desk and wandered on to whichever physician's suite was indicated. And still Elsa sat, drained of any feeling.

Wearily she arose at last. She might as

well get this over with, find a motel for the night, then start back for Chicago on the morrow.

Her decision remained with her until she reached the superintendent's suite. There it ran into a block. The door was closed, locked. The dark windows were proof there was no one inside.

Defeated, Elsa turned and found Dr. Hoag standing there looking down at her.

"I know how you feel, Elsa," he said quietly, "but don't go away. We need you here. I need you — daughter."

2

YEARS Elsa had closed away, memories, swept back as the doctor spoke. She recalled her bewilderment at her mother's decision to leave this man, make a new world of her own in which he did not, could not enter.

Her own father had died shortly after her own birth in a car accident, sudden and devastating to her mother. She had then gone into training, and Elsa's early years had been pleasant, though there were periods of constant emotional adjustment as she was moved from boarding home to whoever chanced to be caring for her mother's apartment when she was at the hospital or on a case.

Then her mother's marriage to this man and security. A place that was always there, an atmosphere of love and understanding.

"Atmosphere," she said, and he

understood. Into the grey-green eyes came a light that had not been there before.

"Here." He handed her a loop from which dangled keys. "The old summer cottage. You always liked it. Not too far away. And, Elsa, perhaps it would be better if you were not identified as my — "

"I understand. I'll rent — "

He laughed. "You would. But all right; see my office nurse after you've viewed the place."

He was gone. For a moment Elsa stood dangling two sets of keys; then she turned in the opposite direction and hurried on to the parking area.

Perhaps there was a divinity which 'shapes our ends,' she thought. Why else would she be here at Port Haven, have surprised Dr. Hoag, then, seeing the superintendent's office was closed, have accepted his offer?

Again the blaze of white light, but this time she stopped for dark glasses, then drove slowly on down avenues lined with palms and oleanders.

She didn't know how she could explain

to her mother. Perhaps, again, by telling the outright truth, something Elizabeth Hoyt vowed was all-important.

The cottage seemed the same, not too out of place among the more modern dwellings, the same shade of tan. And there was that silly stunted palm tree, the one they called Junior. And the same furniture, intricately woven willow. How had it lasted all of this time?

The old-fashioned front veranda had been modified a little, yet it offered ease to anyone with time to sit there.

The door opened. The interior had been repainted, the furniture was different, yet somehow the cottage was the same. All of the squiggly little nerves, like so many worms, which had been chasing each other up and down her spine and even through her head, quieted. This was ease, comfort, security. Why?

Elsa thought of her mother's Chicago apartment with its view of Lincoln Park, the northern tip, and of the lake. Materially there was no comparison. Bob had said they'd have one exactly like it, only, naturally, farther north beyond Evanston.

But why worry or try to compare? Why not rent for a month, and just let down?

She had passed along the slim corridor and come to a rear door, and there lay the 'back yard.' It was the same, except for the phenomenal growth of oleanders which closed it in. Wonderful! What a tan she'd acquire!

Branches parted and a face appeared. "Hello there. I'm Mrs. Ketchum; live next door here. This place is not for rent, y'know. That doctor fellow keeps it for himself."

"And family?" There; the words were out.

"Got none. Don't come much, but when he does he sure lets down."

With you around? wondered Elsa, and thought there was one advantage to apartments or hotel or motel rooms: no one could part branches and intrude.

A further survey showed a thin line in the grass from that particular slit in the bushes. Well, she could take care of that. She might make an enemy, but rather an enemy than an intimate of such as this woman.

"Had him a wife; give her the wrong medicine. She up and died. Then along came 'nother. Married her, but she kept the whip hand and when he didn't jump like as she said, she up and took off. Nobody's seen hide nor hair o' her since."

"You knew her?" Elsa's mind was wheeling.

"Well, no, but heard tell."

Whip hand. Perversely it was in character to a certain extent. Her mother did demand a certain demeanor in others, and rightly so, her daughter defended her. That was the quality that made her such an excellent dean in her chosen profession.

Now try to emulate her. Elsa adopted the incisive tone of voice her mother had drilled into her.

"Mrs. Ketchum, I am a nurse. I have been working steadily but am now on a stand-by basis. I intend to rest between calls. If I seem rude, it is because I consider a patient needs a nurse whose nerves are not tied in knots. It has been nice meeting you. Goodbye!"

"Well," burst forth, "I must say!"

Elsa had no intention of learning what Mrs. Ketchum must say but caught one parting line. "Just wait until Dr. Steffner hears of this!"

Steffner? Yes, she'd seen that name on the rostrum, but hearing it articulated was something else. That blond-haired man with the chestnut-colored eyes. Steffner. And she, Elsa, had been with Jimmy Steffner years ago when his car had broken down and his older brother had come to the rescue.

"Oh, but it couldn't be," she murmured aloud, once she was on the rear porch, converted now to a cozy dinette. Yet wasn't that what he'd said, there in the Port Haven Hospital corridor?

Elsa collapsed into the nearest chair and looked out on dense shrubbery just beginning to burgeon with flashes of white, pink, rose and golden cream. Steffner. Oh, but that had been years and years ago. At least ten, or was it fifteen? Say he'd been seventeen or eighteen or —

"How did I get into this?" she cried aloud.

Well, she was in it, and now to try

either to get out or carry through to a conclusion which would harm no one, herself included.

Elsa drove off. She was really committed to Port Haven Hospital. Until she knew what had caused her mother to divorce Dr. Hoag, he had a certain right to such service as she could give. But she did not have to live in the old 'beach cottage,' so rife with memories of happy days. She would 'view' the apartment Nurse Rawlings had suggested.

She viewed the apartment and for a few moments thought she was back in Chicago, there was such similarity.

Stop acting like an adolescent and get on with it, she ordered herself, and in a few moments was in Dr. Hoag's suite facing his office nurse.

"I would like to rent the cottage," she said, "if it would not be depriving Dr. Hoag of a retreat."

The nurse smiled. "He has bought a small cruiser which does not come equipped with a shore-to-ship intercom. Oh, the name is pronounced as a hoe and an egg."

"Thank you," murmured Elsa, who

had deliberately mispronounced it. "And as I'll be dealing with you — "

"I am Marjory Menkin of John Sealy. I hope you will like it here and, when you're rested, consider full time."

She said Elsa had probably noticed a telephone was installed? She, Marjory, would arrange the necessary change if Hoyt would agree. It could save time, a request from the hospital proper.

"Dr. Hoag said it wouldn't be necessary to have the number, non-listed, changed, but I think it advisable, don't you, Dr. Steffner?"

Elsa wheeled. Behind her stood the man with the chestnut-colored eyes.

"Definitely," he stated, "Hoag receives personal as well as professional calls out there. Miss — what was the name? Ah, Hoyt — might have difficulty screening them."

Nurse Marjory then explained how Hoyt was down from Chicago, Northside Central. She had accompanied a patient down to the air base, and Dr. Crissman had literally talked her into giving them such service as she could while vacationing.

24

"North-side Central," he mused. "Barrington?"

"I've served under Dr. Barrington," Elsa said stiffly, wondering what this man had against her. "In fact — " here her lips insisted upon twisting into a smile — "I specialed his daughter after an appendectomy."

"Hmm. Well, I trust she didn't tell you to get back to a sewing class, that you knew nothing about nursing."

"Ah-well!" came from Menkin as he wheeled and strode off.

"Gridiron," muttered Elsa, and the office nurse looked at her as though she might stride off, or explode where she was.

"It's all right," Elsa soothed her. "Someone must have told him of the act I put on after coming out of an anesthetic. He could have made contact with Dr. Barrington about that time, I mean," she added, leaping from the truth.

Her appendectomy had taken place right here in Port Haven Hospital just before her mother whisked her away to another state. Why, she could at this very moment see this man, this Dr. Steffner,

25

standing at the foot of her bed as she returned to a known world.

And she had thought him his young brother and knew he was supposed to be in Fort Worth at a play-off, not here pretending to be a doctor, a surgeon at that, considering his garb. Ah, that was it. He'd still worn the cap; that was why she had thought he was — what had the name of the young brother been — Jimmy?

Elsa turned quickly lest the office nurse see the sudden alarm she was registering. Dr. Hoag had said it would be better if she were not identifed as his former stepdaughter. And Steffner had so identified her. This could mean her value to Port Haven was gone and, perversely, she now wanted to remain if only to prove herself.

She hesitated a moment. This was really up to Steffner and Hoag. Yet why did it have to happen at this precise moment? With all the utilities on, she had planned to spend the night at the cottage and she was beginning to believe she badly needed rest.

The office telephone rang, and as the

nurse reached for it, Steffner appeared from behind. "Uniform with you? Grab one from Menkin and get down to Admittance." And he was off at a trot.

Menkin didn't wait to cue Elsa. She vanished, then reappeared with a uniform and only then said breathlessly, "A crash on the Causeway access between crowded bus and truck. Bodies strewn all over."

"Which way?" Elsa, who had slipped into the suite proper, now saw several corridors leading from it.

"First to your right, and down." She added, "I'm coming," as waiting patients began pounding on the desk bar. Others coming in had heard of the crash on car radios.

Elsa raced down the corridor, then down a ramp to reach doors swung wide, ready for the low wailing siren's check stop.

"Aide, over here," snapped a voice.

Elsa hadn't time to identify the voice. A second rose. "She's Hoyt from Chicago's North-side Central; doesn't carry her cap in the handbag. On vacation."

Elsa glanced her thanks at the dark-eyed man who had spoken: Dr. Ben

27

Ruark, she would learn. Young, handsome, and, she added, does he ever know it!

Then she forgot Ruark, everything save this glaring evidence of a skeleton crew. That too was swept away as the ambulance doors opened to reveal bodies piled in like wrecked cars in a junk truck.

They were brought in one by one: femur thrust out like the head of a golf club; tibia shafts like sharp knives sliced through skin; a crushed pelvis; and head injuries of every type.

Why here? Even as Elsa charted, she wondered, knowing other ambulances, private and police, had gathered and, where possible, sorted this human wreckage. She wondered until she had a moment or two to watch Steffner. He seemed intent upon some vast jigsaw puzzle, swiftly, neatly fitting of odd bits together.

"Hoyt," said a sharp voice, "delivery room, here."

Elsa glanced up even as she fell into a trot beside a guerney heading out. Dr. Hoag. Why had he singled her out?

And then she understood. A second

ambulance had wailed in, and this baby was not waiting.

An aide rushed ahead to alert one Dr. Bain, but there was little left for him to do when they reached there, and he instinctively patted Elsa on the shoulder blade. "Emergencies do bring out the best in us, don't they?"

Elsa subsided, then braced herself for the great chore still ahead, if that fell to her. Yet another guerney had by-passed them as they'd left Admittance, but it was going the wrong way, the way of no return.

The woman had cried earlier, "We were going home to have our little girl there."

It was a little boy's voice that railed at a world such as he'd entered.

A dark twilight with a bank of black clouds sweeping in from the southwest found many in the cafeteria. Radios and later television had told, then illustrated, what had occurred.

A truck and trailer, heavily loaded, was making its way up the access approach. Behind was the interstate passenger bus, without any by-lane to swing into when the truck's brakes suddenly gave way and it hurtled back on the smaller equipage.

Elsa had slipped out to her car and extracted uniform and cap, had cleaned up as best she could and had slipped into easy shoes.

Now she sat staring at food she'd thought she'd die if she didn't have, wondering how she could ingest it.

Two voices sounded above her.

"This is Nurse Hoyt from Chicago," came Ruark's voice. "Nurse, this is Dr. Hoag, chief of staff. Nurse Hoyt is here on stand-by."

Elsa was standing looking up. Hoag's grey-green eyes were smiling. "She was certainly indoctrinated today," he offered.

Someone called Ruark, but Hoag remained.

"Why did you give me that delivery already half — "

"Hunch?" he asked. "Once there was a little girl with a mother cat. Mother and father of this girl were at the hospital. They returned to find she had delivered seven kittens, tied the cord with silk thread, then, because she had no alcohol to use as a disinfectant, had used what was left of an old bottle of Scotch she'd found."

How could she control her hysteria?

"It worked," she bubbled.

"Definitely," he agreed, "but we had an alcoholic cat on our hands. Refused milk until someone thought of egg nogg with a dash of sherry."

He waited another moment. "I am glad you liked the cottage. You'll spend your rest periods there? If you can take early shift tonight — "

She couldn't, but she would. What was her weariness compared with the suffering of those who'd been brought in?

The food was delicious. Fried eggplant, for instance; she hadn't had that for ages. And shrimp gumbo with prawns; not mere shrimps, but big, fat, succulent prawns. And okra. She'd forgotten there was such a vegetable.

Dr. Bain came in with a tray and sat opposite, "with malice aforethought," he warned.

Hoag had suggested this new nurse break the news of the husband's death to the new mother. He'd stand by, Bains would. They had hoped to put this off until later, but Mrs. Rankin was in excellent physical condition and giving the ward nurse a difficult time with questions.

Elsa bowed her head. How could she? What could she possibly say to tide the woman over this tragic experience? Had she no people of her own? She hadn't. And didn't that make it even more difficult?

"Hoag seems to have a lot of faith in you," Bains continued.

Faith. The key word. "What is her religion?" she asked.

"Some off-beat theory," he sighed. "Comes from southern California."

Elsa nodded and relaxed. Thank goodness she had had a religious complex and studied everything, only to learn they were basically the same, differing mainly in nomenclature.

Quietly then she went to the maternity ward and found, not a woman as she'd previously thought, but a girl.

"Hominy," the girl said fretfully. "I want Hominy. These fool nurses keep bringing me dishes with stuff when — "

"When what you want is Hominy the Hippy?" asked Elsa with false brightness. "You know. How wonderful. Where is he?"

How could she put this into words comprehensible to this girl with a child to support?

"Let's say he had a date with Destiny. He didn't really relate to this groovy world. Let's say he left you a fine young son to see you through, then took off to another dimension."

There was along silence; then the girl sighed. "I really knew it. It's good — for him. That's what counts."

Elsa left her sleeping peacefully. Enviously she looked at her. This young mother felt no bereavement. She would go on with the vivid image of Hominy beside her until another, more material, took his place. And the child?

A nurse could not take on the responsibility of the lives of patients after they had been discharged.

Ah, midnight, and she could go home. Home? Strange that the little tan cottage should give her such a feeling.

Elsa had checked the nursery computer.

33

The baby of Hominy and Helen seemed normal. Now she went down for a snack, there found a nurse whom she had met that evening, and together they did a résumé of the day's events.

"And I said — " began Ruth Dorsey, then stopped. Elsa was staring with unbelieving eyes as a nurse walked in, her uniform, skirt far above the accepted length.

"I don't believe it," Elsa offered.

"Oh, her? Mitzi could appear in a bikini without being criticized, with the *in* she has here."

3

HER *in*? Even as Elsa tried to interpret the term, she attempted to gauge the nurse from her appearance. Beautiful in a sense. Glossy black hair, vivid coloring, wide eyes. But arrogant. She walked as though, if she did not own the entire world, she owned at least Port Haven Hospital.

Ah yes, she was the one who'd snapped at Elsa in Admittance. Elsa had been too busy, too occupied to look at her then.

Now she did and wondered if she had in any way been responsible for the Hoag family break-up. No, ridiculous; the nurse wasn't much older than she, if any.

"Meaning the Chief pampers her?" She put the question with seeming innocence.

"Anything but. If you ask me, I'd say she's like a stick of dynamite, and neither Hoag nor any of the real guys want to touch her for fear she'll explode and blow us all up."

35

To Elsa that could mean but one thing. Without there being powder, there could be no explosion. What was wrong here at Port Haven Hospital?

"Do you have quarters for the night?" Ruth asked.

"Yes, I was lucky. I rented Dr. Hoag's cottage." Again, deliberately she mispronounced the name.

"Man, he must be desperate for nurses. Oh, sorry. I didn't mean that as a reflection on you; just that he's considered that spot sacrosanct. Some say he's still in love with his wife."

"Is that unusual?" Elsa managed.

"Well, they've been divorced for years. She liked that beach cottage better than their town house. And, honey, speaking of that cottage — "

Elsa sprang up. A distant rumble of thunder had alerted Ruth. She raced for the counter where, courtesy of several, there was a large thermos of coffee, a flashlight, a bag of sweet rolls and, she would learn, other delicacies.

"Sure you're not afraid? I mean a new town — "

"I'll tell you tomorrow. I signed up for

four to midnight." And she fled.

She remembered electric storms here, particularly one which had struck a telephone pole on one side of the house, a tree on the other. But this wouldn't be that severe.

Into the darkness she drove, finding it preferable to the blazing sheets of light which distorted the shore highway, made of it a mod — or was it mad? — painting in blue and purple and vast squares of scarlet and gold.

And then when she was beginning to tighten and bend to the inevitable next strike, the cottage appeared and she swung into the driveway, into the carport, and then sat stunned.

Lights had come on in the house, a light overhead illuminating every step to the side door.

A moment later a figure appeared. A woman. Portly, very black of hair.

"*Madre de dios*," cried the woman, "what a welcome to the home!"

"Conchita!" Elsa's voice lifted. Oh, it couldn't be. Conchita Ramos was tiny, or had been. But that had been years ago. Strange how time telescoped. And on

Conchita's mother's cooking, who could retain the form divine?

Conchita was at the car door explaining. The doctor had said Miss Elsa had stayed on to give emergency help. He had called her, sworn her to silence (here Elsa looked at the house next door, and the big woman giggled). *She*, she informed Elsa, would be hiding under the bed.

She gathered bags after that and, both laden, they went in. Elsa practically swooning onto a couch, where she sat savoring the comfort within, the storm without.

"You are not married," Conchita observed, and shook her head. "Me, I am wed to the Carlos Rodriquez in Mexico. Five children we have because of the Dr. Steffner — "

Elsa blinked her eyes. "He delivered — "

No, the Rodriquez had been in Mexico since they married soon after Miss Elsa and her mama went away. Then their eldest, Ramondo, was in a bus, and the bus went over the side. Many were killed, their Ramondo broken into many 'bits.'

The doctors had said he might not live, and if he did he would be a cripple.

Conchita felt if she could carry these 'bits' to Dr. Hoag, he would put them into order. They had managed to charter a fishing smack and cross that part of the Gulf, sneaking into Port Haven to the good doctor, who had taken care of their visas but had said Dr. Steffner could take better care of Ramondo.

"It is the big man who says of a younger he can do better". But now Ramondo was healed in the head and ran with the other boys. Sometimes too much.

Conchita took care of Dr. Hoag's cottage to 'make pay' for the hospital care. She was very happy this was so. And she would also take care of Miss Elsa, but now she must go home. Her Carlos would toot at any moment.

By the time her Carlos 'tooted,' Conchita had brought Elsa up to date on family affairs and warned her against the woman next door. "So full of misinformation." She had also told her, in a most conspiratorial voice, Dr. Hoag had warned her not to let anyone know she had known Miss Elsa before, or that she had been his stepdaughter.

Well, if Mrs. Ketchum hadn't been 'under the bed,' she might wonder at Conchita's welcome.

Bed. Trigger word. Elsa smiled as she made her way to the 'back' bedroom, her room as a child. Conchita had assumed she would use that and had made up the bed; even rigged the canopy of mosquito netting, defying modern day sprays.

Elsa slid in and lay for a moment listening to the thunderous pounding of rain on the low roof and thought its cadence was in rhythm with the thoughts pounding in her head. But she was too weary to sort them.

She arose once when she thought she heard some great street cleaner encroaching, then glanced out of a front window and returned to bed, laughing at herself. She had forgotten how swiftly tropical rains could flood streets; hence the high curbs. A car driving through sent wide wings of water into the air, even as their tires sought adhesion with the pavement.

She awakened to find the sunlight trying to squeeze through the Venetian blinds, glanced at the electric clock Conchita had had the forethought to place within view, then lay back.

Yesterday's impressions — she must sort them, correlate them. Strange how one could go along for months, even years, in an easy rhythm; then suddenly a single day brought more than one could handle at that given time.

There followed a second thought. Need she? Or could she? How many of her preconceived ideas had been tossed overboard in the last twenty-four hours? How could she know what was right? She had proof of only one thing. She, or someone with her capabilities, was needed at Port Haven.

And — she sat up — she had two difficult letters to write, then shopping to do, all before she reported back to the hospital.

In robe and slippers, with pad and pencil and the box the cafeteria staff had packed, Elsa sat at the dinette table. Um, good — the coffee, iced buns and these strange whatever they were: pancakes rolled around sausages. They needed heating.

41

She found the kitchen quite well equipped, and tried to picture her former stepfather concocting a meal. He'd been such a complete loss in any domestic role. Was Dr. Steffner also dependent upon others? Oh, he would have been married years ago.

Interesting, she mused, and flipped a rolled pancake over barely before it became scorched. She considered Steffner's attitude towards her. He seemed to approve of her as a nurse, but acted as though he expected her to explode as a person.

Frowning, she carried the savory viands to the sunny dinette, then sat staring at them. There was something vitally wrong at Port Haven Hospital. What? Would she learn? Did she want to know?

Irritated, she reached for the small table radio and found her mind diverted by a newscast, a résumé of the previous night's highway disaster. Thirty-seven had been involved; five D.O.A. And Elsa's mind switched to Hominy the Hippy and his wife who had sat by his side. Unless he had instinctively thrown his body as a barrier between his wife and the crushing impact, what had determined which should live and which die?

Ah. A question to offer her mother, who had been through these crises times uncounted.

Methodically she wrote then, almost as an afterthought, told where she was why she had accepted and then, how she'd thought Dr. Hoag was not there only to find him chief of staff.

'Mums,' she wrote, 'he looks completely beat inside. When I went back to sign off and found the "soup" gone, he appeared and seemed to know my intentions and said, "we need you." Then he added, "I need you."'

She wrote quite a bit about the cottage. That she'd been told he used it as a retreat until, in desperation, he'd bought a small cruiser so he could get some rest. That she was renting it, for the month at least. That Conchita, now portly, was the maid. Then whimsically she told of the changes in Port Haven.

In conclusion she reverted to the overall thought, 'I sense something very wrong at Port Haven Hospital; possibly

43

economic. I may learn in the short time I'll be here.'

There! After that, writing Bob Latorel was easy. She was having a brief vacation on stand-by basis. She'd brief him after she'd met the pathologists at Port Haven; meanwhile she had to go shopping. Inadvertently she concluded, '*Adios amigo.*'

Now the grocery list. Fun. Did all the female of the species have this instinctive delight in 'feathering their larders'? True, she'd be eating at Port Haven Hospital's cafeteria; or, on off days, at the many places she remembered. Yet suppose she had company. She must be prepared.

Elsa Hoyt, R.N., reported to Rawlings at the proper time, and the superintendent looked at her and sighed. "Now I know the meaning of a godsend. You are it. What is your experience in immunization? Someone slipped up from across the border with typhoid, and we're having a run — "

Elsa shuddered. Somewhere she had been through this, and it was not in Chicago. Ah, Conchita's small nephews had been slipped over the border to where 'Dr. Hoag' could care for them.

"You do speak Spanish," Rawlings remarked, and Elsa knew why she had been isolated. "You can explain."

Explain a practically nonexistent disease in the United States? And why had it struck? And how the patient must be immunized at three month intervals? A safeguard from the typhoid-paratyphoid fevers? Then the educational therapy which must follow.

"My Spanish is pretty rusty," Elsa confessed, and only then wondered how Rawlings could know she, coming from Chicago, could speak it at all. "But I'll try."

Rawlings nodded. "Hoag said you could be trusted. Has a lot of faith in you. Knew him somewhere?"

Elsa waited a moment. "Shall we say, rather, that he knew me, or of me. Well, to the lab?"

"Take this note. You'll find Laisure off-beat in personal contacts but right on the dot elsewhere. His lab work — " she threw up both hands — "phenomenal."

She added, "Now if you'll pick up the Mendozas and take them down — "

Elsa tiptoed back along the corridor to the foyer. She identified the waiting family immediately. They sat, literally huddled, fear plastered across their features.

"*Buenos dias*," greeted Elsa, and was promptly flooded with a torrent of Mexican-Spanish she could barely grasp.

One dark-eyed boy remained silent. Elsa pinpointed him and spoke in English. High school? He nodded. Would he help her by lining up his family, explaining to them this would be no more than a pin prick which would protect them from the fever? Would he assist her? She knew she could count on him.

He grew in stature as she spoke and soon had them lined up to follow her back down the corridor and down a ramp to the laboratories.

"If you'll name each — " Elsa prompted, and importantly he gave the name of each one going up to the medicinal bar, arm exposed.

Only after the last had had his immunization shot did Elsa glance at the technician. He seemed bemused. She would have thought further but again came the torrent of questions, reduced by the boy she'd isolated to a single question.

"What of Maria Mendoza?"

Elsa sent them back to the clinic waiting room and took off to the children's communicable disease ward, where she finally isolated a pathetic small creature who seemed all eyes; great black eyes in a wasted form. Ah, but she had passed the danger mark; the fever was arrested.

Glibly Elsa talked to the small one. An aunt, an uncle and many cousins were here. Soon she would join them. She must eat well, eat 'moch' or should she have said 'muy?' No, the child's dark eyes crinkled at this gringo who so mutilated her language. But she did understand.

"*Muy bueno*," she found herself chanting as she hurried back to ease the family.

And wouldn't Dr. Steffner of all men be standing there, lips pressed together to control a grin?

Happily the family trooped out, and Steffner disappeared. Time now to consider Laisure.

"Would you like to pose a question?" Superintendent Rawlings seeing her preoccupation, posed the question, then added, "Come on." And Elsa followed her back to her office.

"The lab technician," Elsa confessed, "seemed to have a split personality. Only one part was really functioning, the part that counts."

"He's probably blocked off his personal life," murmured Rawlings, "or haven't you met Mitzi? She broke up his first marriage, then, having acquired Laisure, discarded him."

Then, seeing Elsa's look of bemusement, she interpreted it correctly. Why was such a morale destroyer allowed to remain at Port Haven Hospital?

"I don't know, really," Rawlings answered the unasked question, "though admittedly we, and other hospitals here, are suffering a nurse shortage."

Elsa went on to her next chore to assist in relieving a bronchospasm in a patient just admitted. Yes, she told Dr.

Cavitt, she was familiar with the aerosol nebulizer. And — she smiled at him — she also knew if and when to call for help.

Satisfied, the portly little man trotted off, and Elsa went to carry through her duty, relaxing as the man's breathing eased, became rhythmical.

Time for a coffee break. Elsa went down, took her mug and a piece of pie to a far table and sat trying to evaluate what she had heard.

This Mitzi — hadn't her last name been Duval? Then she had discarded the Laisure and, if gossip were correct, an earlier name.

Nurse Ruth had said with her *in* she could have worn a Bikini. That term *in* had to mean she had power over those in control of Port Haven Hospital, or they would never have put up with her machinations.

Dr. William or 'Bill' Bain, seeing her deep study, brought his tray to her table, then asked if she had visited the young man she had helped into the world.

"I looked at him," Elsa confessed. "I

even envied him. He was sleeping, as was his mother."

"We can thank you for that. May I ask you what you said to her to relieve her of her grief?"

Elsa reported, then added hastily she had offered only relief. When realization came, the patient might have a different reaction.

"Right. But meanwhile, what you gave was curative. Now, why the deep study I noticed as I came up?"

Elsa looked at him and could not answer. A handsome man, this Dr. Bain, wavy blond hair, the waves cut short. Grey eyes, young and wary. She also believed every patient he had automatically thought herself in love with him. She was not a patient.

But she must give him some answer. "Oh," she evaded, "just thinking how different this was from the hospitals in which I've functioned. I should think you'd have a waiting list of nurses."

Dr. Steffner came in, in mufti, scowled at her as though she were committing some sin, then began assembling dinner on his tray.

With seeming innocence Elsa posed a question. Was the cooking here so excellent all of the staff preferred dining here rather than at home, or were they merely saving their wives from uncertain dinner hours?

"Could be. Steffner, though, lives at the Yacht Club. If he dines there weekends, it means every member with an ache from toenail to cranium dives in for a free diagnosis. You look a bit tired. Tomorrow off duty?"

"Day after, and then for an indefinite period."

So Steffner was not married. Hmm. And Bain, with something on his mind, went over to join the other.

She'd better start making a shopping list. Dutifully she wrote: 'Swim suit, sun suit, cape.' Elsa smiled, thinking of a woman she'd known. She had come in from a long distance swim, thrown her cape around her, then, on reaching the sea wall, been called down by a policeman for 'indecent exposure.' One shoulder was showing. My, what a shock that man would have these days.

Steffner, seeing her smile and seeing

Bain depart, brought his coffee and pie over. "What's humorous in the world today?" he demanded.

Elsa told him, and he nodded. "These days are better," he informed her gravely. "Even as a medical student soon looks upon the bare human torso without emotion, so will the rest of the world. If you'll check back, you'll find alcohol consumption was limited in scope until the nation went 'dry'."

"'Forbidden fruit'?" murmured Elsa.

"Exactly." Then he added something under his breath that was not complimentary, and Elsa, following his gaze, saw nurse Mitzi walking toward them with a determined step.

"Doctor — " her smile blossomed for him alone; she ignored Elsa as though she were not there — "I have an appointment on Harbor Drive. As you are going off duty, I thought you would be glad to give me a ride."

4

"SORRY," Steffner rose abruptly. "I am heading the other way. I'll call a cab for you." And he was gone.

Elsa recoiled almost physically from the vicious hatred she saw on Nurse Mitzi's face. Then the other swung on her. "What was he trying to put over on you?" she demanded. "He does think he's God's Gift To Women. What was he talking about?"

"Checking on a patient," murmured Elsa.

"Which one?"

Elsa stood up. "It's obvious." She managed a thin smile. "We trained in different hospitals. If you will excuse me — "

"Oh, sit down," snapped Mitzi. "I was only trying to prove him the liar he is. Besides, you haven't finished your pie. Looks good."

It didn't look good to Elsa; a berry pie,

the juice the shade of the other nurse's lips and cheeks.

"When one is as tired as I am — "

"This small duty you've had here, and you're tired?" she scoffed. "And you have that beach cottage to rest in. How did you finagle that out of old Hoag."

Elsa waited a moment, then decided to learn what she could from this nurse.

There must be something to learn. Never had she heard a nurse affiliated with a given hospital speak of the chief of staff in such terms, especially to someone she didn't know.

Truly, Ruth had been right. This Mitzi had some *in* that let her defy even the standards of good taste.

"Very simple," was her reply. "I came here to Port Haven for a rest after accompanying a patient down from Chicago. The only place available was an apartment attached to a six-months lease. I'd agreed to act as a stand-by and was ready to refuse that and return when Dr. — isn't his name, Ho-egg? — well, he overheard and told his office nurse to contact me."

"Oh, well, we are in a spot where

54

nurses are concerned. His fault, too, the old — "

"How is it his fault?" Elsa asked with such interest Mitzi was eager to answer.

"He's such an old fogy we only get the overflow here, like the wreck victims who wanted Steffner; then medicine. Honestly, he's so old-fashioned he won't take a chance on a new drug for simply years."

That could be good, Elsa thought, remembering one outpatient she had known personally who'd had a vicious reaction from a new drug. A month later she was asked to return it, but she had thrown it down the drain without waiting to learn it had been called off the market by the F.D.A.

She had had enough. She glanced at her watch, said she must get back on duty, added, "Interesting talking to you," and left. Interesting but not good. Why, oh why, did they allow this nurse to run loose spilling poison?

Elsa supposed there were those personal enmities in all hospitals, but in the larger ones they were absorbed by numbers.

What an effect this nurse could have on patients if she were vocal, or even allowed facial expressions to convey her distrust of certain medical men.

Intriguing how she'd had an inner desire to spring to Dr. Hoag's defense. Oh well, some day this Mitzi would go too far, and then —

Meanwhile, why had Mitzi had to interrupt her moment with Steffner? Strange. He acted as though he could like Elsa and hated himself for the idea.

Elsa awakened on Monday, slightly apprehensive. This was definitely a day off duty, and she intended to use it as such. The sun was warm; the sand would be equally so. A shift over her swim suit, and she could walk the four blocks due south to the beach. There she would just lie relaxed, unthinking.

Unthinking when she hadn't heard from her mother yet? One wasn't quite sure how she would take any deviation from previously planned procedure.

A letter slithered through the mail slot as she sat down to breakfast, and her coffee cooled as she read it.

'Fortunately,' Mrs. Hoyt had written, 'I could not reach you by telephone at the cottage. I refused to call the hospital. Since then I have had time to cool off a little, though I still do not understand how you reached such a ridiculous decision. Oh, I know: curiosity about a childhood home. But when you learned *he* was there at the hospital you could have shown the good taste to withdraw on some logical excuse. You could have called me, and I would have arranged an emergency of some kind.

'However, now that you are committed — '

Wearily Elsa replugged the coffee urn. This could take boiling hot coffee to wash down.

And then she had to laugh. 'As long as you are there, I trust you will prove your ability.'

Another line had her puzzled. 'I must wonder what kind of mess Paul has gotten himself into this time.'

Elsa shook her head. Wouldn't her mother blow sky high if she were to write her about Mitzi!

And now the letter from Bob. She sipped her coffee as she read. He thought her crazy. Well, good.

If she, Elsa, felt a vacation was necessary, why hadn't she used common sense? They could have married and she spent that time readying their apartment. Now, when could he see her without wasting money hopping a plane two ways?

"I suppose it's the breed," she murmured, half laughing, "trying to put X-drams of income into a test tube and come up with the right answer. Maybe Laisure was like that." Imagine trying to fit Mitzi into anything.

Ah, well, somehow she was relieved. There was that about an anticipated dread occurrence. One had no more illusions and knew how to carry on from there. Well, almost.

At that, it was late in the afternoon before she sought the beach. Lovely, she thought, spreading a rug, tossing her light cape and bag beside it. Not too many here. She had been warned not to seek an isolated spot. There had been what were called 'incidents.'

She'd forgotten the peculiar blue of the sky and the water, the froth of waves. Truly, this was worth any discomfiture she might suffer at the hospital. She would swim until she was physically tired, then come out and take a small dose of sunshine. Not too much; her skin might erupt in revolt.

And the water was as warm as she remembered. Happily she dove in through the first breaker, then faced the next and the next. Wonderful.

She was through the surf and into comparatively calm waters, relieved her old Australian crawl was still functioning, still shooting her forward easily, when she heard a sputtering roar from behind.

Treading water, she turned.

"Are you out of your cotton-picking mind?" demanded the prone figure behind her. But as he'd submerged, she could not identify him for a moment.

Then he came up. Chestnut brown eyes glared at her, and she glared back.

"I do have a distance record in these waters," she informed him loftily.

"Complete with a school of sharks?" he demanded. "Head back and fast. They're just surfacing due south."

Elsa headed back, fast. Sharks? My word, had even the gulf waters become enemies? Then she remembered another incident where guards had made such a whirlpool of waters these enemies of the deep had backed away.

And wouldn't this happen when he of all persons was around?

They stood up on the shore, and he subsided. "Look, Nurse; first you check with lifeguards before you go out too far. They have copters casing the seas."

They made their way up the beach to where she had left her rug and bag; then she, toweling her hair, was brought up to date on swimming procedures.

"You always swam around the piers, right?" he asked. And when she nodded agreement, "There were always boats and many swimmers, and the denizens of the deep avoided that area. Down here — well, look."

Both scrounged their heads down as brakes screamed a protest on the avenue above; then there was a metallic smack, and the car lodged nose in to the curb.

Steffner was off at a run, Elsa behind him thinking, if she thought, he'd witnessed something she hadn't. He had but not what she thought. When she pulled up behind him he was literally gritting his teeth at the woman behind the wheel.

"'s'all right." She beamed. "Gotta take the shillern — "

Elsa looked at the children. Only the younger of the three seemed amused; the other two, especially the boy, about nine, seemed white and frozen.

"Della," Steffner was saying, "you're in no condition to drive. Why, why, why do you risk it?"

Momentary sobriety struck. "What have I got to lose?" she asked.

"If Bill catches you like this, the right even to see the youngsters — " Then, aware of Elsa, he introduced her as a stand-by nurse at the hospital, down from Chicago on a so-called vacation.

"Hoag sent me out to pull down some garden furniture he had stashed under the carport roof. He was on his way when an emergency came in. Afraid she'd try to knock herself out."

Elsa looked at the woman and smiled. "My, don't they have a lot of confidence in us! Why don't we all go to my garden for a cookout?. I'd love having you. I think there are swings and things — "

"Right," agreed Steffner. And to the woman. "Move over; I'll drive. Nurse, you take my car."

Elsa almost saluted. Instead she ran back to the beach to gather up her and the doctor's personal effects and load them into his car.

Thoughtfully then she drove off. Bill. Oh, this couldn't be Dr. Bain's recently divorced wife. She was a sick woman; surely a physician would see that and attempt a cure. And why did Mitzi's face loom up before her when she was no place around?

Bet she has a hand in this somewhere, Elsa thought, and pulled in behind the other car.

"Keep your eye on her," Steffner said softly as he came up to the car, purportedly to check on whether or not she'd picked up his things.

62

Keep an eye on her? Elsa, seeing Steffner mount an inset ladder, looked up. There she saw a mass of aluminium tube-framed garden pieces with plastic webbing. Good; they dried more quickly than the willow.

Della Bain, for so she had been identified, had taken Elsa's invitation to 'come in' seriously and quickly. When Elsa reached the interior, she found Della and one child missing.

"She took Stymy to the bathroom," the middle child, a seven-year-old, informed her.

Stymy, who was Stanley Myron, reappeared, but it was several moments before his mother followed, and Elsa wondered just how far a hostess could go to keep an eye on a guest. That large bag she carried, for instance.

And the guest? She seemed re-enforced physically, but her speech had thickened, and she wavered as she made her way to a deep chair and sank into it.

"Why don't you go in and lie down?" Elsa offered. "The children will be helping me with the cookout."

For a long moment hazel eyes searched

63

hers; then came a deep sigh. "Why not? They'll never miss me, and I want the besh for them."

"She's lying down," Elsa told Steffner when he came in from aligning the furniture in the rear garden. "I suggested it."

"Good. Now what do you need? Market's not too faraway."

"Let's let them choose."

They wanted 'Long Johns,' which proved to be wieners in extra long buns with 'globs' of 'goop.' Elsa reduced this to what she had on hand, and Steffner drove off for the prime ingredient.

He returned with a 'plop pool' guaranteed to keep the children amused after they had finished eating, and the wieners.

It could have been fun, Elsa thought wistfully. Even the frozen white-faced boy relaxed a little. Yet all were conscious of that other member of the party inside.

"Willis — " they were through eating, with a promise of ice cream later — "you teach the others how to throw a ringer so they won't plop. Right?"

"Yes, Dr. Steffner, but is Mom going

to have something too? She ought to be hungry."

Steffner looked at Elsa. "She was more tired than hungry, Willis. As soon as she awakens, we'll see she has a full course dinner."

At the utility porch, as Steffner helped her carry food into the cottage, Elsa stopped. "Can you brief me so I won't hurt the children?"

Steffner placed his load on the small table and breathed deeply. "I don't know. Who does? As a pediatrician, Bain can't be beat. As a psychiatrist? He lifted his arms and dropped them. "Around three years ago, Della began turning from a social to a steady imbiber. She put on scenes at the Country Club that made everyone dread to see her come in. Above all, she began neglecting the children. The youngest was a baby at the time.

"Finally, when the life of the eldest had been risked, Bain divorced her. She's allowed to have the youngsters one day a week. After today, I wonder if that is wise."

"She won't 'take the cure'?"

"As I understand it, she won't admit

65

she needs it. Well, let's brew some coffee black and stiff and see if we can give the kids a break. And I have to get back."

Elsa smiled. "Thank you for coming to my rescue."

"Hoag said you never asked for help in anything you thought you could do, even though it might mean landing in a hospital as a patient."

That was one way to impersonalize, thought Elsa, and her chin went up and out.

He glanced at her, rapped, "Better get some lotion on, fast. You're baked," and strode into the bedroom after a slight knock.

This time it was Elsa's spine that was affected. Obviously graciousness was not one of Dr. Steffner's assets. On the other hand, she thought, after a startled look at her facial skin, he was honest. One would always know exactly what he meant and on that basis could act accordingly.

It didn't work with Mrs. Bain. Steffner came out, shaking his head. He couldn't 'get through to her.' Elsa was to try.

"Looking like this?" she protested,

aware her sheath was colorful and currently matched her greased face. "I'll tone down and don a uniform."

"Don't," he ordered sharply. "She feels such instant revulsion at the sight of a uniform she could stagger out and take the youngsters with her. Now try. I'll risk waiting another few minutes." And he strode to the rear garden.

Della Bain was sitting up sipping coffee when Elsa entered. She was a pathetic figure, a woman who had been, if not beautiful, very attractive.

"All right." She sighed. "Get on with the lecture."

"Lecture?" repeated Elsa. "About what?"

"What I should do. What I have done wrong. Why. How — if I'd done as they said — ad infinitum." She waited a moment. "Take half a dozen good friends with 'your best interests at heart,' concede they've meant well, but what do they do to you?"

"The ones that work on me," Elsa confided, "confuse me so much I do the wrong thing."

"Then you're not — "

Elsa shook her head. "Even if I'd

known you for years, knew your background, your problem from all sides, I wouldn't venture an opinion. If I considered you worthy of being my friend, I would also concede you had the intelligence to work out your own problem. More coffee?"

"Why not?"

Elsa found Steffner ready to leave. He had called 'Harbor' and was needed. He'd take the children, deposit them at home. Would she? She could take a cab back from wherever Della was staying.

With Steffner and the children gone, Della Bain said she'd enjoy a bite of food. Willingly Elsa took her to the dinette. And now that she had combed her hair and used a bit of make-up, Elsa could better judge the ravages of her emotional distress.

Della brought them up. How did one readjust to taking the wrong advice?

Elsa hesitated. "One friend said she'd be blessed if she'd let others crow over her, and made a comeback. Then there was another who'd been through so much she suffered extreme nervous exhaustion. She moved away to a place where sights and sounds wouldn't trigger a nervous reaction, until she was strong enough physically to ignore, even laugh at them."

Still Della waited, and Elsa sighed. "But of course first comes evaluation, learning where one went wrong in the first place. And by wrong I mean took the wrong attitude plus action."

"There have been times," Della said softly, "when I thought of suicide, of making them suffer a little of what I'd been through."

Swiftly Elsa picked this up. "Then you awakened to the realization that would prove them right and you wrong. Even your close friends would concede there must have been a little something offbeat with you all along."

The startled look convinced Elsa she had been right in saying this. Yet, having spent months in Emergency, she knew how often this could trigger an attempt at self-destruction, a desire to make someone else suffer.

"People who are self-centered enough to destroy another's desire to live are too self-centered to believe they are guilty of anything."

Della nodded. "I'd better get home. Would you — I mean I'll call a cab. Somehow now I think I see a gleam."

Swiftly Elsa picked this up. "When you're completely down and defeated remember that. It takes a little while to build the body so your spirit can enjoy life."

Della reached into her bag and carefully wrote down all that Elsa had said, underscoring the last, then adding titles of books which would help her along the way.

The telephone rang, and a voice asked Elsa if she could report to Port Haven Hospital within the hour. She said she could and was told it would be only short duty.

Then Elsa turned to Della. Would she destroy the effect of all she had said if she admitted to being a nurse? Or would it be better that Della learn now than chance running into her in uniform later?

5

"THAT was Port Haven — " Elsa began, and Della Bain nodded. "Then you are not surprised to learn I am a nurse?"

Della laughed faintly. "Would Al Steffner have dared bark at anyone but a nurse as he barked at you?"

No, she hadn't thought of Elsa as a nurse, a saleswoman, or anything else as they talked. "You were being yourself, completely honest," she explained. "I've been around enough of the other kind to spot them."

"Wonderful," Elsa cheered. "You're a long way up the road. Now me, I have to be hit over the head and dragged through the mud before I can be convinced 'such nice people' have ulterior motives."

"You don't want to make me over?"

Elsa's curls danced as she shook her head. "I am having trouble enough straightening myself out without checking to see if you need making over. Maybe you only need to be your real self."

At the carport Della hesitated. "I can drive all right now," she said. "That will save you from taking a cab back from the hospital. Trust me?"

There was a strong hand clasp, and each started toward her own car. Then Della turned back. "You forgot something. You didn't tell me to weigh what you'd said."

Elsa's laugh rang out. "I don't even remember what I said. Whatever it was, you sparked it, so it's in your lap."

Della nodded. "One thing! Would you mind following me? I'd like you to know where I live so if I ever grow desperate enough to call you — "

"Will do."

It was a high-rise apartment in the heart of the high-rise residential district. Expensive, Elsa noted. And at the moment it was quiet, with no other cars around. She waited a moment, then looked up at the apartment Della had indicated and saw the lights flash on. Della Bain was alone again, she and her thoughts. What devastating company they could be.

And now for Port Haven Hospital. Elsa's car spun along even as did her thoughts. Everyone else seemed out searching for fun. But Della must weigh and use such advice as had slipped through her lips.

"Oh, Hoyt, good girl," came a greeting as the ward nurse checked the clock. "Sorry to call you in, but Mitzi had a heavy date. An alcoholic friend sent a distress call. Unable to drive her children home." The older woman shook her head in distress. "Such a pity."

"Oooh?" Elsa's question asked for more data.

"The woman is indirectly affiliated with the hospital, so naturally there are those of us who keep an eye on her."

"A former nurse?"

"Well, no."

Elsa glanced up. Steffner was standing well back in an aperture of doors and windows leading to the main office. She raised her brows slightly, and he answered with a nod.

Mitzi Duval, then, had gone to the

rescue of Dr. Bain's ex-wife and children?

"If you'll check that emphysema in four-ten — "

Elsa took off at a trot, but Steffner was not far behind.

"I delivered her to her apartment quite sober," she reported. And, "I like her!"

"Right. The children too were safely delivered. Incidentally, did Della make any calls out?"

"No! I had the telephone moved to my bedroom. She was never in there."

"Consider that," he advised, and went down the corridor.

Only the rigid training she had received kept Elsa from obeying Steffner's orders. One concentrated upon the duty at hand.

Yet there came a time when she was free of personal care, of preparing dosages for individuals, when she might allow her mind to return to the afternoon and evening.

If she hadn't been in my own home, and had I not been right there with her, she thought, I could have accepted that story. Now all I want to know is what the not so fair Mitzi carried with her when she went to the so-called rescue.

What had she told Della about evaluating situations and people? Had she evaluated Mitzi? Perhaps wrongly? No, that fake call established that.

And while you're about it, she told herself, just ask yourself how you got mixed up in this situation.

Mitzi came in at midnight, brimming with importance. She had, she let raised brows convey a meaning, 'taken care of the problem.' Children were tucked in at their home; the problem was 'sleeping it off.' A shake of the head; she would now complete Elsa's duty.

Elsa went back through quiet corridors. Steffner, called back by a surfer who hadn't anticipated a loose log as competition, saw her leaving and hurried out to make sure she had her car with her.

"I am betting on her," Elsa told him defiantly; "that is, if someone didn't get to her after she reached her apartment and was admitted." She hesitated a moment, then asked, "But why?"

"Oh, what's the quickest way to be rid of competition?" And he was gone.

Competition? Did Mitzi want Dr.

Bain? Who would not, considering his charm? And if she did, what quicker way than to destroy even the last memories Bain held of Della?

Elsa drove past Della's apartment house to find her apartment dark. Ah, well. But as she entered her own door, a flash of white at the sill stopped her.

Cautiously she picked it up to find an envelope with a handwritten letter inside. Anxiously she took it in to a low light to read.

'I don't even know your last name, so I can't write you from where I am going. But I thank you for talking sense to me. I have made my choice. I am starting for my home city the minute someone gives up trying to reach me and her car drives off. I have an uncle who will see me through. He'll also arrange to have my things packed and shipped so nobody can pick up my address. He will also talk to my attorney.

'I don't expect to be free of "things" immediately. But I do feel right with myself for the first time in years. I know if I ask, you won't tell anyone where I am.

'But will you ask Albert to tell the children mama, who's been sick a long time, has gone away to recover so they can have fun again?

'Della.'

Albert? Oh yes, Dr. Steffner. And it would ease the children.

Elsa sat a long time holding the letter, thinking of Mitzi, the poison she had spread with innuendoes. What could be more vicious? In time it would recoil on the liar, but meanwhile the lied about must suffer.

She had laid the envelope on her bedside stand when she noticed a note, an afterthought?

'You're so right,' Della had written. 'Our senses do trigger unpleasant memories as well as pleasant ones. How long before I can stand the thick sweetness of oleanders without heartache?'

Which means, Elsa thought, she's moving far from this area. Interesting; in her they induced a feeling of peace and security. People were so alike and so different. Take Mitzi. Elsa supposed they were literally stuck with her.

Again her mind returned to the old question. Why did the hospital allow such a person on its staff?

And Steffner. He could have caught the desk nurse with her innuendoes and thrown them back at her as lies, where she, Elsa, couldn't.

True, the nurse had mentioned no names. Well, he could have demanded a name, couldn't he?

Maybe, Elsa finally let go, he's just waiting until he's sure 'the calf has enough rope to hang her.'

She slept late. When she awakened, she lay feeling as though she would like to purr. Now any normal person would have been instantly alert, even frightened. Elsa giggled. Conchita, who'd been around the cottage for years, was still bumping into the corner of the low drain board and calling on her maker to appease her pain and anger.

I'll swing a bell, Elsa thought, remembering a friend's mother who went about with lumps on her forehead because she couldn't learn to duck beneath a basement rafter — until her husband swung a bell just inside the door. One jingle and she ducked.

Conchita tiptoed in, wheeled, hit the drain board, spoke earnestly, then returned with a tray, carrying a bowl of Rio Grande grapefruit, pink and delicious.

No, Elsa told her she'd enjoy this here but have breakfast outside.

"One eye closed in milk?" Conchita asked.

"I'd like that," Elsa cried, thinking back to her return from her appendectomy. Her mother had left her there with Conchita, who looked askance at a bland diet.

"Little pigs in brown jackets?"

"Wonderful. My appetite grows with every word. You fix what you think I'd like. I'll be out within fifteen minutes."

She was, but not in the sun suit she'd planned to wear. This south Texas sun really ate into one until the skin was toughened to its caress.

After she'd relaxed in the webbed chair Elsa considered the wisdom and sprang up to warn Conchita the next door neighbor might be listening, to say nothing that would let her know they had ever met before.

Conchita did even more. Addressing her with pristine formality, she added, "Miss Nurse maybe should put the barbed wire in that hole in the hedge." There was 'one on the far side who does not know the body; she needs rest. Only the tongue she herself works.'

Stiffly then she marched back to the cottage, leaving Elsa and her poached egg and sausage; a hysterical Elsa.

Perversely her mind returned to Della Bain, who had also returned to familiar scenes. She supposed no one could make a complete return yet she hoped Della could have as much relaxation as she herself was having, based on the response of her senses to the peace and happiness of the early days spent there.

Peace? Ramondo came roaring in with a power mower, and Elsa fled into the house to find Conchita roaring around each room she sought for quiet, armed with a vacuum cleaner.

True, this would happen only once a week. Meanwhile, where would she go, what would she do?"

Be sensible. Ramondo wouldn't spend the entire day in the back yard. He didn't. But when Elsa sought asylum there, she found the submerged watering system activated, and the retreat was filled with rainbows — wet ones.

Elsa had lunch on the former porch, Venetian blinds closed. Proudly Conchita brought in a platter of *Enchiladas de Pollo* and stood by to await Elsa's reception of this creative art.

One bite of the stuffed tortillas, and Elsa was silent. Conchita had prepared them, seasoned them, as she would have for her own family, not for the *gringo* Elsa had become through the years.

Elsa wiped the tears from her eyes, and happily Conchita nodded. Elsa, she said, had remembered. She had. Some place within these rolled pancakes she would find green peppers and tomatoes, chopped grapes and green olives, and chicken. But she couldn't isolate the chicken with this lovable woman looking on. Nor could she say she wasn't hungry.

Perhaps if she just plowed stoically on, her tongue, esophagus and stomach would be burned to insensitivity by the intense heat the spices generated. Or perhaps Conchita would leave.

Conchita wouldn't think of it. She would dust, after she and Ramondo had had their *enchiladas*.

And Elsa would also lunch because she, she told herself sternly, hadn't enough character to tell the maid the chili peppers were literally burning the lining from her insides.

A few bites. Better. Now she could taste a little. Doggedly she went on and suddenly found a delicious tidbit.

Her mind whirled. Of course. Weren't all native dishes based on conformity to needs? In southern climates near the equator where man originally depended upon man-made insulation from heat, the danger of tainted food was reduced by such seasoning.

And in time the body adjusted. She hoped hers would.

"Medication," she said aloud.

"You sick?" Conchita asked.

"No, goodness, no. Just thinking." And the woman beamed and left her.

Even as one became accustomed to

such seasoning, so could a patient become so accustomed to certain medicines they were no longer effective, or effective only in ever increasing dosages. Elsa went on with her theory, splicing it occasionally with conjectures on how much additional time it would take Conchita to finish.

Then she gave up. With Conchita there to answer the telephone, should Port Haven call, she would do what she had been wanting to do: drive the length of the island, acquaint herself with any changes.

Camera at the ready, she got into her car and set forth into the already blazing early afternoon sun.

She'd find a cool spot, have a cool drink. Cool spot? And was there a car following hers, or was it her imagination? Why shouldn't someone have pulled out immediately behind her and be heading in the same direction?

She'd see. She had a little trouble with new one-way streets; then achieving a right one, swung toward the waterfront.

Then she wished she hadn't. Great trucks with trailers spoke to her lowly car in horned language one couldn't help but translate. There was nothing she could do to comply with their demands but duck if and when a space appeared.

Ah, the wide busy road was turning away from the deep channel wharves. And she was tense. That long pier ahead. She remembered it as a spot for a cool drink, or port for a light boat at the foot of the pilings.

There were many boats there now, lifting and lowering gently. Their owners were on shore earning their upkeep, Elsa imagined. There was also parking space; a rarity, she assumed. And here came that low yellow car.

"Taking the doctor's cruiser out for exercise?" asked the man driving.

"Which doctor and what cruiser?" Elsa retorted. "Frankly, Dr. Ruark, I noticed a car I thought might be tailing. I'd had one bad experience in Chicago and tried to check. I took the wrong turn and landed in truck traffic."

"And stopped here?"

"The sign says: 'Cold Drinks.' I need cooling off after that battle of the fenders."

"Diagnosis accepted. Cold drink

indicated. May I?" He'd come to her car and now held the door open.

Elsa was glad she'd worn a conservative frock, not from choice but for protection from the sun's rays. Her body proper was red and raw enough from yesterday's initiation. Lack of concern over her appearance was going to be an asset in the questions and answers game she felt was imminent.

"I see you took our climate too seriously," Ruark remarked when they were seated at an east window table. The soft breeze and slap of low waves were a relief after the hot drive.

"Or ignorantly? I didn't know the sun was turned onto high this early in the year. I cooked."

"Then came out in it again today, I suppose you had a good reason."

"I thought so," she retorted, remembered this was a doctor and she a mere nurse, and if she intended to remain at Port Haven Hospital she had better watch her words. "The woman who comes once a week to clean the cottage was cleaning. Her son was mowing and watering the rear garden lawn. I wanted to relax, so I started out seeking an eastern exposure, shade from the sea wall if any." Did she dare ask, "And you?"

Ruark nodded. "I waited around a bit for her to clear. I was down seeing a patient; thought I'd drop in and become acquainted. I have a theory a doctor-nurse team can work more efficiently if backgrounds are established."

No one could have looked more guileless than Elsa at that moment, with light brown curls fluffed by the sea breeze, grey-blue eyes wide and eager.

"I'd just love knowing all about you," she said wistfully. "Imagine finding someone like you here in this comparatively small city."

That hadn't been his intention, she thought, watching his expression change swiftly from austerity to bewilderment to pride.

Dutifully he gave his training experience, a little of his family, Middle West, and then, almost unaware of his words, painted the great dream which still lay ahead.

Elsa had a ridiculous vision of a driver in a circus parade, a man who gathered all of the horses into a single team and now sought to drive them from the high box seat where he perched trying to hold the reins, jerk each steed into perfect coordination with the others.

To Ruark, she thought, doctoring was Big Business. Running a hospital was acting as owner-manager. Patients were X number of shoppers who came into purchase services. And the more you sold them, whether or not they needed them, the more successful your business.

No wonder the nation had become a contorted version of its original intent, or could, if such as this man held the reins.

Suddenly he stopped and stared at her. "I rather let go," he admitted. "There is that about you. I assume your patients also — "

Elsa glanced at her watch. "Oh, my goodness, the time," she whimpered. "I have to get back before what's-her-name leaves. Why not come along with me, and I'll — "

"If I didn't have an unbreakable date, I'd suggest I bring a garden dinner to your current residence. Another time?"

"Fun," murmured Elsa, feeling like a feminine Judas. Then she added, "Your unbreakable wouldn't — " How did she know intuitively it was Mitzi Duval?

He shook his head, smiled and said he'd slip in when others weren't watching, then, ushering her into her car, drove off.

Swiftly Elsa turned her car west and speedily drove a main boulevard to come at length to the small tan cottage.

She had no more than turned in when a portly woman came running toward her, a child of perhaps two in her arms.

"The pills. He said, 'Pretty pills.' He swallowed I don't know how many. Now look at him."

One look, and Elsa raced for the telephone, wondering if there would be time to save the child.

6

THE ambulance having been called, Elsa barked at the operator. She wanted Dr. Hoag immediately, regardless of what he was doing.

In the short interim she turned to the wailing woman who had followed her in.

"What pills?"

"Like rainbows."

"Diet?"

"Yes."

"Put the baby here beside me. Now bring that brown bag. Oh, Dr. Hoag, Nurse Elsa." And swiftly she relayed the information, adding she had called an ambulance.

"I have syrup of Ipecac here. His age?" The mother answered. "Then a teaspoon — yes, immediately."

Even as she trickled the emetic into the throat of the almost comatose child, Elsa wondered why parents did not learn emergency procedures for their small ones.

Elsa glanced at a small girl who had followed her mother. "Can she find the pill bottle?" And when the child had been ordered to hurry, "Do you know how many it contained? How many you have taken?"

Elsa looked up in relief to find Creighton, an intern, bending over the now retching small one; then her gaze returned to the contents going into a white bowl she'd slipped in swiftly.

The basic color at the moment was the brown of the ipecac, but within one lump was an undissolved pill —

"I'll follow," Elsa said as the baby was carried to the ambulance. I will bring the pills and little girl." And then, "How many did you take?"

"Just the one," wailed the mother over her shoulder. "There were fifty, I understand. The doctor had just left them for me."

Left them for her? What doctor?

Elsa scooped the baby's older sister into her car and gave her a small box she'd picked up en route.

"You count while I drive. Count ten at a time."

"Mama tried to stick her finger down Dodie's throat," the girl defended her mother, "but he sorta choked. 'N she'd heard you were a nurse."

Later she said, "There's sort of forty-two, but some spilled on the floor when Mama grabbed Dodie." And Elsa gave up.

One thing about this derivative of wild fox glove leaves: its effect was cumulative. If they could rid the small body of its power in time, he had a fighting chance.

"What was that awful stuff that you gave Dodie that made him sick?"

"Something every mother should keep in her cupboard," Elsa replied. "Ipecac." And she tried to describe the effects of this syrup, the alkaloid of a Brazilian root which could cause the stomach to empty quickly.

Ah, the hospital. How comforting it looked to Elsa. Swiftly she parked and hurried in, the phial of pills in one hand, the hand of the small girl in the other.

Dr. Hoag was just coming up from Admittance, and Elsa handed him the phial. "No prescription visible when this young lady brought it to me."

"I'm sure I recognize it. Take it to Laisure. A more accurate estimate of the digitalis." And he hurried on.

Laisure looked up intently and, after Elsa's relay of Dr. Hoag's words, grunted, "Providing the same amount is in each capsule. Stand by."

It seemed to take forever, especially with the anxious little sister watching, but eventually came a qualified report. Minimal was the word used after Laisure had given the result in percentages.

Elsa, her immediate duty over, sought the mother waiting anxiously. Dodie seemed better — his color, for instance. Then her voice arose in self-defense. She always kept medicines far above the reach of small ones.

A diet pill hadn't seemed poisonous (neither did a simple aspirin). It was, Elsa sought to explain, a case of dosage versus the bodily size of the one taking it.

"Out of the mouths of babes?" asked a sardonic voice.

Elsa wheeled and found herself staring at a tall, black-haired man who seemed to encompass all of the arrogance man could carry.

"Oh, Dr. De Horenston," breathed the mother, "how is he? Will he — " She couldn't say 'live' and she couldn't say 'die.'

De Horenston, thought Elsa. So this was the second-in-command at Port Haven Hospital. He had been off on a cruise, 'taking a much needed rest,' since her arrival. No wonder Dr. Hoag looked as though he were the one who needed a rest if he had to work with this person.

"We cannot give a definite answer as yet. And this — " He flicked a hand at Elsa.

Swiftly she spoke. "I am here as a neighbor, not a nurse, Dr. De Horenston."

"You are the one who gave the child — "

"Only after clearing with Dr. Hoag by telephone."

"Did she do wrong, Doctor; did she harm Dodie?"

He shrugged. "Probably saved him." Then he strode off.

"Isn't he wonderful!" breathed the hysterical mother.

"Is he the one who gave you the — "

"Oh, my, no. He's too famous to bother with anything like overweight. Here comes Duncan. You can go now; he'll take us home."

So much for being a neighbor, or a nurse, thought Elsa, as a harried-looking businessman rushed up, asked about his young son, then began explaining how difficult it had been to charter a plane and, upon landing, to find someone to drive him to the hospital.

At the turn of the corridor Elsa found Steffner. "You are not indignant," he remarked.

"If a child's life had not been involved," she returned, "I would be laughing. That night in Houston when Dr. Crissman decided I should come down, I overheard a remark he made: that the nursing profession was one that wouldn't be computerized. Frankly, Dr. Steffner, I am beginning to wonder if there aren't patients who consider us robots."

Steffner nodded. "Good girl. That attitude could save a lot of people a lot of medical bills and perhaps save our time for those who really need it."

He was off, and so, she reasoned, she had better be, both physically and mentally, turning over the events of the day to a file marked past and accounted for. Yet was it?

Driving home, the question kept nagging at her. Suppose she had been elsewhere under the same circumstances, been unable to reach a physician. She would have been faced with a decision. Even knowing the properties of a drug, just how far dared a nurse go when a child's life, or an adult's, was at stake? A mother, knowing what the child had ingested, yes. A neighbor who chanced to be a nurse?

The little tan house looked like a real haven. The back garden would be shady. She'd place the telephone on the bedroom window sill and then relax.

Or would she? Turning into her driveway, she had a memory flash of backing out earlier, and shortly afterwards noticing what had proved to be Dr. Ruark's car. Had he been the one to leave the diet pills?

And what business was it of hers?

That, she thought, finally sinking in to the coolness of the ribbed reclining chair, "is what makes life here so different from life in Chicago. It's personal and emotion-involved."

Ah. Elsa relaxed, staring up at the now rose-amber sky. How swiftly this day had sped along, and how much had been encompassed within the hours.

A moment later she was sitting up. She hadn't answered Bob's last letter. Nor her mother's. Nor did she want to write to either at the moment. What would she say in answer to their questions? Why anything? Why not simply tell them what had occurred?

Elsa leaned back again. Strange. It was just a little lonely here. That was one difficulty for a person in her profession. Unless one made a careful choice of confidants, one couldn't 'talk out' the tensions of the day.

She supposed she must have food. Reluctantly she scanned her shelf of canned wares and the refrigerator. A jar of chicken and noodles. She had enough chicken left over from the take-out to give it authenticity. Fruit in lieu of salad.

How quickly twilight fell down here. She had forgotten and stumbled a little making her way back to the webbed chair. She should have sat before the auxiliary television and had her mind diverted.

From the next yard came voices and delicious scents of barbecued beef.

Then one voice rose, and Elsa forgot barbecued beef and chicken and noodles. Mrs. Ketchum was really holding forth.

"There he lay, flat on the floor, right in the middle of this club meeting. Everybody just plain knew it was a heart attack, though he'd never had one before. So they called his doctor. Know what?"

A moment's silence.

"That man, that physician said, like he didn't give a care, 'Well, bring him over.' And his club members were afraid to touch him lest they do the wrong thing. They figured calling an ambulance might take too long, so one of them called Dr. Hoag. Eating his dinner he was. And in nothing flat he shot over there like he wasn't plumb worn out, and gave first aid.

97

"Now that is a doctor, a real physician. Didn't ask no questions; just heard a fellow being had a need and shot right over. Didn't even stop to figure was he trespassing on another doctor's territory. All he knew was the need, and he answered it.

"Folks say the fellow will live on account o' Dr. Hoag."

A moment's silence; then a sardonic voice mutters, "Maybe more business for Port Haven Hospital?"

"Not him. He's got all the patients he can handle and then some. No, it's some of them others trying to take over who're giving that place a bad name."

The phrase, 'some of them others trying to take over,' seemed to Elsa to stand out, illumined. True, Mrs. Ketchum was called Misinformation, yet perhaps she had inadvertently sensed what was going on at Port Haven Hospital. Ah, more talk.

Eagerly Elsa began eavesdropping.

"This woman called her neighbor and sorta gasped she was dying, to come quick. The neighbor called the physician. He said yes, the woman had called him

98

first. Then this neighbor said what should she do? Know what he said? 'Call the coroner and the sheriff.'"

"What happened?"

"Well, this neighbor woman she shot over there and gave the medicine the woman pointed at, but she was too far gone. She died. So then the neighbor woman called the coroner and the sheriff's office, and was she ever put through a grinder."

"She'd have died anyway," muttered one.

"Possibly," agreed another. "But wouldn't she have gone her way in greater peace, knowing help was forthcoming, had the doctor taken a different attitude?"

Perversely Elsa's mind swept back to another overheard conversation. Had people become so many robots to be computerized? Dr. Hoag still saw them as individuals, as did she. And up to the now starry sky went a prayer that she would never become so inured to her profession she saw only bodies, not the individual spirits that animated them.

Darkness lay deep over the tan cottage

before Elsa remembered the chicken and noodles. But there were two letters ready to be air-mailed to Chicago. And if her mother didn't approve of what she had written about her former husband, that was just too bad for her mother. She had written the truth.

As for Bob: well, there was one thing about a lab technician. They could see only 'cause and potential effect.' They were vitally necessary in determining a given condition, yet did they lift their sights above a 'patient's name'? Did they view that name as an individual with a life, with others dependent upon it, with the potentials of the individual?

Elsa reheated the chicken and noodles and forced them past reluctant lips. The fruit went down more easily, yet now she could better understand a patient's refusal to ingest food when the living of life seemed so confused, so questionably worth-while.

The next day dragged by on leaden feet. Well, hadn't she wanted to rest? How could one rest, she asked angrily, when something somewhere seemed about to explode?

She'd return to Chicago immediately. Well, not immediately, but within two weeks. This heat seemed weighted down, a physical force that flattened even the spirit. The garden was too steaming hot for comfort. She would burn to a crisp on the beach. She could shop, but for what? Maybe she should attempt to check on old school friends. But she couldn't under present circumstances.

A pale, half exhausted woman appeared at the door. Mrs. Narston, she said was her name. The doctors thought Dodie was out of danger unless something occurred. What could? The nurse didn't know? Then why did doctors always have to take such a gloomy out look?

Swiftly, automatically, Elsa sprang to the defense of medicos. Each case was individual; unless a physician were psychic he couldn't foretell what reaction might occur.

"That Dr. Hoag" had given her a bad time, Mrs. Narston reported. "He tried to pin me down to find out who had given me the pills. As though I'd tell."

"Then you accepted them, knowing

they were not approved by Port Haven Hospital?"

"That Hoag may seem like a good landlord to you, but to a lot of people he's just an old reactionary."

Elsa had had enough. She stood up. "You can say that after what happened? Had Dr. Hoag not tested that particular pill through the Port Haven labs, he could not have given me permission to give the emetic. And Dodie? Good afternoon."

Elsa closed the door against the heat and the now awakened woman. Let her suffer awhile. Maybe then she would awaken to the brainwashing she had received from someone, either the person giving the pills or an associate.

Imagine them trying to turn even this against Hoag!

I simply must stay on until I learn more, she thought. I'd never forgive myself if I didn't. Did Dad realize that when he asked me to stay; when he said they needed me, then added he needed me?

Yet how could he have foretold her reaction?. Perhaps, she sighed, he'd been desperate enough to snatch at any straw.

From the front view window Elsa looked out on the bay waters, now turning slightly amber. A cruiser idled along, heading due west. Why didn't he simply get into his, stock it up, take off and never return? Most men would.

But not a dedicated physician who was aware how many patients associated his diagnosis, his ministrations, with well being.

"Say it out loud," ordered a voice.

Elsa looked up, bewildered. She had somehow stalked through the house to the rear garden, possibly because she had become aware someone was out there.

And there stood Dr. Albert Steffner in mufti, long fork carefully turning, of all things, liver sizzling gently over low coals.

"They cook it to leather," he defended himself, "and we don't get enough. About tops the list of anti-anemia and anti-stress foods. Now you were saying? Stop looking around; I brought everything."

"I was saying there were too many medical men who believe they belong to the latest, the highest aristocracy the world has ever known. They think they're so far above the lowly patient, said patient should salaam on sight."

"Go on."

"They live in the most beautiful homes, belong to the best clubs, have the finest cars, yachts — Oh well — "

"Yet you are not convinced?"

"The greatest medical man I ever met was the most humble in the last analysis. He had genius of mind and fingertip. Then one night came an emergency, a patient he'd never before met. The patient died. And he sat, head bowed, saying, 'where did I fail?'"

"Another tried to assure him he hadn't failed. But he couldn't quite accept it. Not through conceit but — oh, well, you've perhaps known — "

"My Waterloo was a little girl who'd been struck by a car. No visible reason she shouldn't have lived; I felt somehow, somewhere, something had slipped past when I wasn't watching."

Elsa grabbed the long-handled fork and saved the meat, which was beginning to sizzle. Then hurried in for plates that would hold the halved potatoes baked in foil; the finely chopped coleslaw, the lettuce and tomatoes she added, topped by a piquant sauce.

They sank into comfortable chairs, small tables straddled over the arms, sighed, then dined.

"Used to come out when Hoag was here," Steffner confided. "Pretty fine being able to ease down with his — " He hesitated, then continued, "Not everyone I feel at ease with."

Elsa sighed; 'At ease with.' Well, she supposed that meant something, though she wasn't sure what.

What had spurred this invasion, Steffner continued, was a report on the Bain children.

It hadn't been easy. *Someone* — he emphasized the word — had talked to them. The eldest had said stonily his mother wasn't sick; she was 'a drunk.'

And how had he handled that? He'd said, as a doctor's son, the boy must know what could happen when one was forced to take the wrong medicine, or even talked into it. That had struck fire. The boy had thought for a while, then nodded and said, "I read you."

Steffner believed the boy had even identified the one bringing the 'medicine.'

"Tough on him if she becomes his stepmother," mused Elsa.

Steffner grew rigid, and Elsa wondered why his extreme repugnance at the thought. He couldn't be jealous, could he? Then she saw him sit straight up and found head lamp reflections bathing the oleanders to the east.

A moment later Dr. Ruark stepped through the small gate. "Imagine finding you here," he greeted Dr. Steffner.

7

ELSA felt she could see the enmity of the two emitting sparks in the dark garden.

"Oh?" Steffner spoke casually, "You and I have met here before, haven't we? But I was not aware Nurse Hoyt had an appointment with you." He paused, wrinkled his handsome nose and added, "With roast chicken a bonus?"

"What was your contribution — barbecued beef? A side? Nurse, you must have been well fed."

She was, she might have said, 'fed up' to have two professional men acting like teenagers. Instead she suggested they go indoors; it was growing 'a little chilly.'

Promptly Steffner said he must leave, if Ruark wouldn't mind backing his car into the street to allow him to exit? Ruark gave a cry. "Man, delighted." And Elsa, after one appealing look at Dr. Steffner, turned away.

And she'd thought she was lonely

earlier. Which was preferable: being alone or trying to observe protocol in such a situation?

When she turned to take with her a load of soiled dishes, she found Dr. Steffner stonily stacking grill plates and silver, even as he might have cleaned an incision area after suture.

"I think," Elsa breathed thoughtfully as Ruark's car roared into action, "if I intended remaining here, I'd have a nurse or businesswoman to share the cottage."

Steffner set the grill plates down with a clatter not in character. "Excellent idea. I could stay on. However, there's that old cliché — 'the sooner the better.'" And suddenly he was gone.

The sooner the better? Oh, he meant the sooner she isolated what he'd have called an infectious bacillus, i.e. Ruark's intentions toward herself, the better for her.

Ruark returned, looking thoughtful. "Hoyt, I'm sorry I barged in as I did. I recognized Steffner's car, but I'd no idea he'd take that anxious father attitude toward you. How did he classify me?"

"How would I know?" she evaded.

"He's not particularly communicative. But then few physicians are."

"Now how about this chicken? Do I have to eat the whole thing?"

He had pulled the portly bird from its wrappings, and she had to laugh. "If you can hold it, do. Here, let me find you a platter and a plate. Dinette acceptable?"

"Definitely."

An hour whisked past on wings, Elsa spending most of it laughing at the man across from her. There had been no further personalities involved, and no questions.

"Good to be free of shop talk," he said eventually. "Here, put this poor old hen in your refrigerator. And this lemon pie, what's left of it. Good, wasn't it?"

"Early duty tomorrow. Imagine you'll have a call, too, the way things were piling up when I left. You and your vacation," he teased, then sobered. "Not that you look as though you needed a rest. Truly, why did you come down?"

"'The truth, the whole truth and nothing but the truth,'" she quoted solemnly, "Dr. Crissman took me by surprise. And I had no valid reason for refusing."

"Your family?"

"I think Mother is slightly envious. Being dean of a nursing school isn't exactly relaxing."

His chin came down, and his expression changed. She wondered if he had been entertaining suspicions about her presence at the hospital; above all, her presence in this cottage. And was he now satisfied she was not a Hoag devotee?

As for herself, what had she learned? Nothing. Ruark could be utterly charming. Steffner? She'd had a ridiculous feeling when he'd spoken of the select few with whom he felt at ease. She had longed to have him around, always, to provide the ease.

Above all, did these two 'Mighty Men,' as some young nurse had called them, always carry dine-outs to new nurses?

Anxiously Elsa scanned herself in a mirror. Not bad. The crimson was paling to tan; the colorful shift had helped. Yet she was no *femme fatale*, and she knew it. Was it simply she was someone new? Above all, someone from out of town?

Of course Steffner had identified her. It was possible he had hoped to extract confidences from her, learn how she felt about her former stepfather, how far she could be trusted to carry out any plan he had in mind.

Oh, go to bed, she ordered the pink-cheeked girl in the mirror. And surprisingly, the girl obeyed, taking Elsa with her.

Not that she slept well; she was back working on her decision problem.

And it was gusty outside, and cloudy, she noticed. Rain indicated? Chilly, too. Crazy weather. One thing about Chicago: one could count on the weather 'being consistently what you don't want.'

She had reached for the telephone before the clamor of the first bell died. Yes, indeed, she'd be glad to report in immediately.

Elsa made a record dressing and reaching the hospital. Weather again? She wondered as an ambulance droned in.

A nurse on duty at Admittance had slipped and twisted an ankle. Nothing serious; they wanted to keep it that way.

The first guest entered in the arms of an intern, screaming. Behind came the guerney, the mother asking wildly, "is she all right, or he — I mean is the baby — "

The ambulance attendant gave her a dour look. "With those lungs, Madam, prepare for a new star on your horizon."

Half an hour later mother and child were cleansed and calmed and occupying different beds. Elsa returned in time to assist as a burly longshoreman was brought in and filled the air with a new and colorful vocabulary.

That was what came of being on the midnight-to-dawn shift. That blasted crane had bared its teeth at him, swung down, grabbed him by the leg, then tried to hoist him back aboard. And him no seafaring man, not since the last war. They could have their — he slowed. Something else had bared a sharp point at him, eased the pain. And now he was being rolled away to the X-ray laboratory.

Elsa took time out for a coffee break. Dawn was slow in arriving, the clouds thick and black outside. She'd barely been served when the alarm light went on, and she raced back to her post.

A young teen-age boy with a ruptured appendix.

They talked together, she and the boy, as they awaited test summations.

At a nod from the acting physician, she walked beside the guerney as he was taken in for emergency surgery. She had learned in the interim that his mother had been unable to face accompanying him. She was afraid she would break down, her fears intensifying his own.

Two days later Elsa would call on him and be given a humorous story. He had thought he was made of stone and there were strange men hacking at the stone, yet all of the time he could see her standing there, nodding, approving of what these others were doing. 'Sure made it easier,' he would say.

And Elsa, by then disturbed by other problems, found solace in this boy's humorous account of his operation. If she, as a nurse, had made such a crisis easier, then truly, what else was more important?

After a lapse of time, she found herself

studying the night staff, men she hadn't met before. She liked them. They were there, as was she, to ease, rather than pose as authorities.

A call came in on the intercom, and promptly all were alert. This was a police call. Car off the road. Man slumped over the wheel. Ambulance indicated? Hold everything.

"Some pulse," came a sharp voice.

"Cardiac," snapped one of the men behind her.

Now came a sharp argument. One officer was starting artificial respiration.

"The idiot," wailed a voice behind Elsa.

She wanted to cry, no, it wasn't idiotic. These men were like the ones her mother had told her of in McMinnville, Oregon. There, a man, who would become the chief of police in time, was faced with a mysterious death. He had cared enough about his work to take extra courses in the effects of carbon monoxide on the human of the species.

He had found this woman sitting at a table in her home, slippers on, relaxed. There were only two empty beer bottles nearby, and they were dry enough to have been left for some time. No gas heaters, no other burners, oil, or closed fireplaces which might have given off deadly fumes.

In time, steadily pursuing the case, he checked back on her activities of the evening. We learned she had sat in a car, with the heater going, and a faulty muffler, gradually imbibing deadly fumes as she talked to the one with her.

Perhaps there had been a 'few drinks,' but her blood content revealed point twenty-eight alcohol and, topping this, thirty-five of the deadly carbon monoxide. And the man, her car companion, had taken his suffering emotionally. He hadn't known, hadn't realized that the effect of alcohol and carbon monoxide was as deadly as that of alcohol and tranquillizers.

"Some response," barked the voice. "Pulse accelerating."

"I knew it," breathed Elsa, and the entire staff turned on her.

"Don't you see?" she pleaded. "Police trained in this type of emergency can save many lives. Too many, finding someone slumped over the wheel, cry cardiac or coronary. True, they can't carry labs in their hip pockets, but if they are trained by dedicated men, they can know if and when to take the chance of respiration and, if necessary, heart massage until the ambulance reaches them."

One man ran his hand back over his brow. "And I have never given the police credit for anything more than picking up criminals."

"You should meet Chief Wayne Lofton of McMinnville," murmured Elsa darkly. "He knows how often it is the police and not the medical men who first come upon an emergency."

In another moment she was saying no, they were not trying to take over the medico's job; merely to keep the individual alive long enough for the man with the better medical knowledge to take over.

Next she added the most vital information. Police such as these were trained to check the car immediately after calling the ambulance. Then, and only then, if there was evidence of a faulty vent or muffler, anything channeling carbon

116

monoxide back into the car, did they act.

The patient having been brought in and put under oxygen, in time the emergency staff went down for a coffee break, plying Elsa with questions she was only too eager to answer.

Many cities, she said, had their traffic men watch for evidence of faulty mufflers on the streets and highways, then give a warning. The majority were teen-agers with older cars, as yet unaware of the lethal fumes they carried about.

"I remember one up north," remarked an intern. "Cold evening. Couple went out on a date, sat it out, motor going. We were able to save the boy. Not the girl."

By the time Elsa was off duty, the heavy night rain, which had nearly cost a man's life as he tried to seal his car windows against its onslaught, had stopped. The sun came out, steaming and hissing at its competitor, and Elsa anticipated a real tropical day ahead. She'd sleep through the worst of it, after she had faced a new decision.

She had been in Port Haven long

enough to decide if she were going to remain any length of time. She had been at the hospital long enough to know there was something vitally wrong there, but not long enough to determine what it was or whether her presence would assist in straightening it out or further complicate the situation.

Swiftly now she reviewed the two doctors who had called on her the same evening. Suppose Ruark had arrived first? What would Steffner's reaction have been? That was easily answered. Finding Ruark or anyone else's car there, he would have turned away.

Suppose Dr. Hoag had agreed to slip in for a much needed hour of relaxation. How would Ruark have reacted?

Elsa shivered at the thought. Had that sophisticated young medico found them alone, in the garden, who knows what he would have read into it?

"I have to have someone here with me." Elsa spoke aloud. "That is, if I intend to remain."

Should she? Bob's letters were becoming shorter, more impatient. Her mother's were longer and contained more pertinent questions than news; questions she couldn't answer.

Well, just how could one with no valid reason for asking demand the financial situation of Port Haven Hospital? Her mother had a better chance of obtaining an answer to that than she.

Elsa had received pay covering her 'periodic duty,' a comfortable check which made the days between seem more like a paid vacation. But she couldn't continue indefinitely on that basis.

Perversely, Elsa found herself padding around in the rear garden as though an answer might pop up out of the greensward in full bloom. And in a sense it did.

"Men. I hear their voices. Girls? Humph, with her looks, why should she waste her time on girls? Well, if you ask me, she's no better than she should be."

Elsa's shoulders shook. How she loved that cliché. Who was? she always wanted to ask.

"Dr. Hoag? Hmm. Well, could be he'd rent quicker to a pretty young thing. Always did have an eye out for that kind, I'm told. Folks say some nurse was angling before him and his last wife busted up."

Now Elsa approached the hedge with the stealthy step of a kitten stalking its quarry. Such a situation would have had more effect upon her mother than anything else. But had the other nurse won? Like an answer, came the voice.

"Who, her? Nope. After money, I understand. Married an oil man. Deevorced him first chance. Hear he was so glad to be shut of her he made her a fat settlement. She took off on a spendin' spree. Nobody roun' here's seen hide nor hair o' her since."

Elsa chose the front bedroom for the doubtful rest ahead. At least the sun wouldn't be beating at that wall all day.

Dad should have had this set up with a ventilating system, she thought, then was shocked at the term she had used. Dad. She must stop thinking of him that way. It could slip out and ruin everything.

Ruin what?

Irritably she pounded a pillow, drew a light sheet over her and settled down. All right; she had reached her decision, for the simple reason she couldn't look forward to going through life elsewhere with this nagging question riding her shoulders.

"I'll invite some of the girls down from Chicago for vacation; that will solve the having-someone-around problem."

She would have a bit of a nightmare. Men were in the garden. First Bob Latoret, scorning it, planning vast improvements which would consist of buying up all nearby houses, razing them and then building a high-rise apartment. Their home would be the penthouse on top. Nobody could listen in on their quarrels.

Quarrels? Ruark had appeared. 'Why bother? I just walk off and let them stew.'

Then came Steffner's voice. 'First the diagnosis; isolate the factor creating the quarrel.'

She'd never know what followed; the telephone brought her up groggily. She managed to knock it from its stand before she made proper contact.

"Hoyt? This is Rawlings. Do hope I didn't waken you. I've been awake for weeks. Building going on next door to my apartment. Hoyt, can you come in for a conference? You can? Fine; I'll be in here until four."

Elsa glanced at the clock. Goodness, she'd slept longer than she'd realized. And she was still tired. She needed coffee.

The pot plugged in, she reached for note paper and dashed off a line to Dorothy Alberts. Dorothy could enjoy a vacation here, regardless of what Rawlings had in mind, she could stay on another month in this cottage, couldn't she?

Deciding she might as well find out what the superintendent wanted, rather than sit there and stew, Elsa appeared at Port Haven Hospital at two, looking like anything but a nurse.

"Cool," said Rawlings wearily, referring, Elsa hoped, to the pale green and white suit she wore. "Sit down, Hoyt."

"Before you say anything," Elsa spoke hurriedly, "would you consider taking a rest break at the cottage? There are fans there, and it is quiet. Honestly, I don't know why I'm saying this."

A smile appeared. "I do, Elsa, but I don't want to intrude. Your mother never felt that way. Yes, I've finally identified you. And I shan't say anything further. I would enjoy an occasional let down at your place.

"Now about you. If you are rested, we would like you to consider remaining on here until after the vacation period at least, on a full time basis. As you know, summer is our busiest period. It is also the period when our help rightfully expects time off."

She waited; then Elsa nodded. "I think, subconsciously, I'd hoped for this. Yes, I'll stay on."

"As you know, we rotate duty. If you'll start four to midnight tomorrow."

Elsa wafted down the corridor, but not far. From out of somewhere came a beautiful young woman in white, cap sitting atop her head like a tiny cloud.

"Oh, Hoyt, you answer to a maiden's prayer. Could you — would you let me rent quarters from you? I've been evicted. I mean, they're razing my building, and I've stayed out the limit, and this time of the year there simply is nothing else.

I'll pay. I'll pay well."

My, what charm, thought Elsa as the dark-eyed girl beamed at her. But this I do not want in my home. Or do I?

8

MITZI DUVAL waited only a moment, then cried, "Hoyt, you look shocked. Surely — "

Surely what? thought Elsa as the other stopped on that word.

"I am shocked," Elsa replied evenly. "I've just mailed a letter to a Chicago friend telling her she was welcome to spend her vacation here. She has a younger brother stationed near here, one she's concerned about. As your need is immediate — "

"Well, not that immediate," parried Mitzi. "When is her vacation period, and for how long? I could find something temporary."

"I haven't any of the answers," Elsa replied, frowning, "but I imagine she'll give them in her next letter. As for the length of time she'll stay," came shrugged shoulders, "she may do what I did: take a leave of absence. I'll let you know as soon as I hear."

"Why can't you wire?"

Elsa stiffened. "We trained together, worked together. A wire would make her think I didn't want her. And I do."

"More than you want me as a steady diet?"

"You said that; I didn't," Elsa threw back at her with a smile.

Dr. Hoag chose that moment to move down the corridor. Looking at him, Elsa frowned. He seemed to be dragging one leg after another. His face was gray, drawn. As he neared he looked from one to the other, seemed to hide a frown, nodded and passed on.

"Some of these days he's going to crack up," Mitzi confided. "Then we will be in one unholy mess."

"Oh? Why?"

"You don't know much about this place, do you?"

"I am here as a nurse," Elsa returned. "My interest is focused on such patients as are allotted to my care. I don't even know the name of the business administrator; who owns the controlling interest. And somehow I don't care. To me none of this is as important as caring for — " She stopped.

Rawlings had shot out of her suite. Attention focused on Elsa, she said, "Ah, you haven't left . Would you take Admittance? Could be third degree burns; ambulance on the way. Duval, aren't you supposed to be on Nine?"

Elsa's immediate thought was thank goodness she'd been given a locker and could swiftly find uniform, shoes and cap therein. "See you later," she told Mitzi, and went off at the fast trot her big city hospital had developed with its miles of corridors.

She couldn't think, she wouldn't think of the problem Mitzi Duval had posed. This poor blackened body must be relieved of clothes burned into its skin, its flesh.

De Horenston, on duty, won Elsa's grudging respect. He barked orders with the assurance of one who knew they would be obeyed instantly.

Swiftly Elsa worked, anticipating the orders. For hadn't she been one of the many to serve when a school had burned and patients were brought in, not one by one, but by the half-dozen, until every emergency and admittance room was jammed.

Ah, there. De Horenston made a final check before the patient was wheeled on to intensive care; then he turned to look at Elsa. "Not bad," he stated. "Not bad at all."

And again she had the ridiculous idea she should salaam. How could a man with such healing genius in mind and finger tips be so arrogant? Above all, what was he doing there at Port Haven Hospital, an edifice under some shadow which must restrict his work?

Elsa changed to street clothes and headed back to the little tan cottage. Time now to consider Mitzi's astonishing request. "Request my eye," Elsa muttered. "Demand."

Yet she could not keep her mind on Mitzi. Memory of Dr. Hoag and the way he had looked as he passed them kept flashing back.

The moment she reached the tan cottage, Elsa went immediately to the small desk and began pouring it out to her mother. 'Honestly, Mums,' she wrote, 'I don't know whether it's because I once called him Dad, or because I'm seeing him as a nurse sees a patient, but he looks ill, exhausted. I can't understand why some of the other physicians don't demand he take a real rest.'

There was a postscript. 'Mother, should I know our "soup," Ruby Rawlings?' And she related their brief personal talk.

Sealing the letter, Elsa thought: One thing about remaining on. Those at the hospital were falling into classifications, the pro Hoag and the Con Hoag and the indifferent or comparative newcomers.

Tired as she was, Elsa took time to wander through the cottage, envisioning Mitzi Duval as co-renter. Or would she ever be co-anything? Wouldn't she adroitly take over the running of everything, with the possible exception of Conchita? Mrs. Rodriquez she'd probably try to discharge once she'd found she couldn't be 'brought to heel.'

In her bedroom, Elsa stood in the doorway. Some letters had blown from her night stand and lay scattered on the floor. Now if Mitzi were there, they would be neatly piled or banded together, and who was to say they would not first be read?

I wonder if I could stand having her here, she pondered, with Bain, and who knows what other doctor, calling on her. Elsa had noticed not too many of the nurses seemed friendly with Mitzi.

Well, this decision took more wisdom than she was generating at the moment. She'd take a complete rest, such as she'd enjoyed during student days.

It was well she did, for her new duties started within a very few hours, and they proved the business of healing could not be forecast as could other forms. There were slow days, then days so crammed with duties it seemed impossible to tamp them down into a given set of hours.

She had thought she would be on Admissions and was until a call came from Rawlings. Would Hoyt hurry down to the lab and prepare for extra duty on the communicable disease floor?

Going in for her immunization, Elsa studied the face of Laisure and wondered how he liked working around his former short-term wife. Or had he some means of immunizing himself against any emotional reaction?

"What's happening?" she posed the question.

"We'll know soon. Malaria or infectious hepatitis. I'd say the latter. Rash of it broke out at a resort with its own water supply. Fewer incidents, might have put it down to yellow jaundice. Similarity."

And, thought Elsa, the latter can grow out of the former. Well, she braced herself for heavy service. She had had only one case of this type before. It had meant constant watch of temperature fluctuations; biopsies; repeated changes of bedgowns and linens and reports on effect of food consumption. And there would be a challenge to induce the patients to eat small but frequent meals, replacement of nourishment which had been scourged from their bodies.

She met Dr. Hoag just beyond the lab doorway.

"You were in there for — " He glanced at her arm. And he was angry.

"It's all right." She caught herself

131

before she said 'Dad.' I've had shots, and I've handled this before. I will be careful. I know how which is half the game, isn't it?"

He nodded; then, aware of others approaching, "The nurse — "

She knew he meant Mitzi. "Not my dish of tea," she murmured, and he seemed relieved of some portion of his load and hurried on.

Elsa, taking the elevator rather than the escalator to the tenth floor, overheard a few pertinent remarks between an orderly and a nurse's aide.

"Hoag hit the jackpot on this one," the aide remarked.

"He's tops in this area on tropical disease."

"Hepatitis is no geographical disease."

"True, but there is a relationship. Then, too, with his experience in the tropicals, he can more quickly isolate and confirm."

The girl shrugged her shoulders. "Want to bet he won't use the latest lab-tested medication?"

The orderly took a quick look at Elsa, who seemed to be staring straight ahead.

132

"If I pick up the bug, I'll be happy if he waits until it's tried out on a few others first."

The aide stepped out on the next floor, and the orderly gave Elsa an apologetic glance. "Six weeks, and they know more about their profession than someone who's been in for six years."

"And are more outspoken?" queried Elsa. "I've only served in rather large cities where — "

"Admittedly there's a laxity here, but who knows what to do about it?"

She left at the next floor and went thoughtfully down to where a patient was being wheeled in, a drab-looking woman who surely had been beautiful a short time before.

But that was the scourge of this disease. Until many reported the same conditions, it was often attributed to other and individual causes, from incipient appendicitis to tainted food.

Rather like Port Haven Hospital, a disease so insidious it must become acute for correct prognosis?

Dr. Hoag hurried down the corridor, and Elsa picked up her step. At least she would be working under his direction for a change.

Carefully Elsa listened to the orders. Intravenous injections of alternate glucose and saline solutions to replace sugar and salt drained from the body. Then a steady check of rise and or fall of temperature. On and on, a routine familiar to Elsa, though she had never seen a patient so exhausted by the disease, and wondered if Dr. Hoag had made the initial error.

Eventually she learned the patient had tried to 'sit it out' at home, thinking it was something she had eaten. Then her husband, back from a business trip and realizing her condition, had hurried her off to Port Haven. By then the drama of her admittance had pricked others who had been thinking they had 'seasonal diarrhea.'

Only a few required hospitalization. The County Board of Health had been notified and before the day was over had found a cracked water pipe imbibing waters from a slough which had been catching run-off from the inadequate sewer system of the little resort. As this was ordinarily a 'poor man's disease,' not too well known among the resort patrons, it had not been anticipated.

Interesting, working with a man she had called Dad and who, when she was small, had eased tears and bruises as he held her on his lap.

Now he was cool, impersonal, and once snapped at her so irritably she nearly jumped in response. A motion at the doorway. Someone had stopped there. He'd been aware of it and deduced she would be better protected should he snap than if he showed even normal doctor-nurse courtesy.

How quickly this was proven. Her dinner break was late, the nurse shortage acute. Yet that was indicative of Dr. Hoag's standing where this disease was concerned. Patients preferred being brought to Port Haven Hospital.

She chose food at random and sat in the nearly deserted cafeteria only to find the aide who'd been in the elevator bearing down on her.

"Oh, boy," the girl offered, "let anybody, just anybody, man or beast yak at me the way Hoag bit into you, and I'd give him what-for."

"Oh?" Elsa looked up. "You should try a big city hospital, though I doubt you would be accepted. There, as obviously here, it is the patient that is important. I am quite sure Dr. Hoag, like any other physician, saw me only as a pair of hands that had fumbled. Now if you will excuse me, I have notes to take."

She made notes and dug her pen into a scratch pad, the results going on to her mother. My, wouldn't she take the wind out of the sails of a girl like this one!

Four nights passed. The patient, Mrs. Grayson, was now taking soft foods that would line the tortured intestines. The fluctation of temperature had abated; the exhaustion, too, was giving place to interest in what lay around her.

The other patients, their infection caught more quickly, antibiotics immediately going into war against the baccilli, were being readied for discharge.

Outpatients also fell off in number, practically everyone within the resort radius having come in for immunization.

Elsa had caught occasional glimpses of Ruark, few of Steffner, as surgery was by preference an early program.

Ruark managed to pop up at unexpected moments, yet — and Elsa smiled — he did not come too close, though hepatitis germs were not purported to fly through the air, unless transported by mosquito.

Dr. Bain looked in twice and would have chatted with Elsa, but his timing was off and lights flashed, calling her to respond immediately.

She puzzled only a moment, then thought: naturally, the children would have talked of that evening at the tan cottage. He would want to know what had been said by his former wife, perhaps to refute it.

And that, thought Elsa, is why Mitzi has shown this interest in me.

"Wonder how she is getting along," mused Elsa, and like a quick reply, received a letter the next morning.

The friend who had arranged transportation for her personal effects had been asked to learn Elsa's full name and the cottage address. Mrs. Bain wrote frankly, she would not trust some who might handle the mail at the hospital. And Elsa cringed.

She was doing 'quite well,' Mrs. Bain

wrote. Her uncle had taken her to a psychiatrist, and he had awakened her to the fact she had 'allowed' herself to be manipulated by a designing woman. She could trace it back step by step. She had been 'cured' of her hatred for this woman; that was replaced by a form of contempt for herself.

'Admittedly the woman is dangerous, but I am supposed to be comparatively intelligent. I watched her work on her Great Scheme and felt smug, never realizing getting rid of me was part of that scheme. And that, my dear nurse, is a form of conceit. Now my sole interest lies in reclaiming a little of what I have lost. Self-respect is first on the list.'

My, what an emotional catharsis she had had.

It was Conchita's day on duty. She came in looking first worried, then sly.

"Maybe you like the little pick-up this morning?" she asked.

Elsa stared at her, puzzled, and from behind her back Conchita brought forth what was left of a fifth of whiskey. "You work hard," soothed the maid. "Maybe — "

"It must have been left here." Perhaps by Mrs. Bain. She wondered.

Conchita shrugged. "She not here last week. I find her first shelf."

Dr. Hoag had keys to the house. Rawlings? She had slept there. But no, not Rawlings, who was bitter against anything alcoholic due to a family tragedy.

"Conchita, something tells me new locks on the doors are indicated."

Conchita gave an explosive "*Si*" and trotted off.

"And a post office box for mail," Elsa added to herself. She shuddered when she thought of her mother's mail she had left neatly stacked in the desk, then smiled. Nothing could have been more misleading, more impersonal. How wise. She had even spoken of Dr. Hoag as 'that chief of staff you mentioned.'

But Bob's letters! She ran her hands through her curls. Oh my, oh my. On the other hand, maybe that was good. He never referred to anything but their plans for the future, his annoyance at her for extending her so-called vacation.

No, Bob's letters would definitely establish her as a temporary nurse who had felt she must answer a call of distress.

Yet that invasion of privacy, the most cherished of all American rights, bothered her, and swiftly she wrote to all who had been corresponding with her, carried the letters to the main post office and obtained a box, then added the number before mailing her expressions of indignation.

A line from Della Bain's letter pounded at her. 'The Great Scheme.' What was it? Hoag knew and was helpless. Why?

Take the hospital. Even those who Elsa believed to be working with the 'other side' performed with amazing efficiency in their profession. No patient could possibly suffer from the inter-staff disharmony. Suffer physically, that is. On being discharged, they might carry some implanted prejudice against Dr. Hoag.

Well, she thought happily, next week she would be on midnight to dawn duty, and the snoopers would have to stay up or rise at a more difficult hour.

Returning from the post office, she caught a far glimpse of the hospital and slowed. Why this decision to stay on, try to see things through? What made her think she was smarter than her mother had been? As for Dr. Hoag, how could a mere nurse possibly correct a still unknown condition where he had failed?

She carried the question with her all day, working it over pro and con, weighing the outcome. She could lose Bob by what to him would be dereliction of a love-duty. She was certainly losing financially, paying rent in lieu of living at home. And for what? She could also end up in some horrible situation which might cost her her reputation.

That night she looked at Dr. Hoag making his late call on the few patients left in the now called Hepatica Hall. Then automatically she fell into step with him, jotting down orders.

Nearing the corridor door, she caught a glimpse of a particular person, and her voice came sharp and clear. "Dr. Hoag, would you mind if I had new locks placed on the cottage doors? Your maid Conchita and I have found evidence of prowlers."

Hoag glanced at her, then at the door from which the figure had now disappeared, and smiled. "I'll do better. I shall make the replacements myself."

9

AS Elsa might have foretold, Mitzi was in the cafeteria when she went down for a moment's rest and refreshment. But by then Elsa had been fortified by a quiet chat with the doctor, the first they had ever had.

"I'll bring Steffner along," he had said. "We three can match dates. I could hire someone for the locks, but his deft fingers and quick thinking could add something a locksmith might overlook.

"Now your next time off duty? Tuesday. Fine. Will arrange. Then the three of us can go out to dinner."

"Oh, please, couldn't I prepare something and we have it in the garden? We can dine out any time, but this — well — "

"It will be a real occasion, won't it, Elsa? Yes. I think we will both enjoy that. Rather like old times," he added softly, and hurried away.

Elsa was busy, mentally working over

a menu, and didn't see Mitzi at first. Hoag was of British descent. Now what had he preferred above everything or anything else? Ah, roast beef and was it Yorkshire pudding? More important, did she remember how it had been prepared? The batter was poured around the base of the roast when it was nearly done. Ah, but what were the ingredients of that batter which came out golden brown on top, rich with juice beneath?

"My word, girl, you do need a housemate." Mitzi slid in opposite Elsa and set down her tray. "I heard you asking old Hoag for new locks. Honeychile, why Hoag? Who else has a key to the ones you have on?"

"Are you saying it was he who made illegal entry?" Elsa asked with disarming innocence.

"No, I didn't actually say that. Just use that pretty head of yours."

"Good idea." Elsa nodded. She'd do just that. First, she'd ask how Mitzi had been shifted to this duty so suddenly. "Imagine seeing you here at this hour," she began. "I thought you abhorred the old night watch."

A shrug of shoulders. "Just a night or two I can take. We're running short as usual. Honestly, this hospital — "

"If you don't like it, why do you stay?" Elsa still seemed innocent of guile. "I mean, this shortage is national, not confined to Port Haven. Or," now she smiled, "is there someone special here you're af — I mean unwilling to leave behind?"

"Not necessarily; I just do not like being pushed around. But seriously, Hoyt, what have you heard from your friend? I could really use a little relaxation in your back yard after a tough day here."

"Oh, then you know the place. I haven't had time for a reply, not really. Not unless there was a rush, and I indicated none when I wrote."

"Well, why don't I move in until she shows up? Then I can find temporary quarters elsewhere until she leaves. Meanwhile — "

"You said you did not like being pushed around." Elsa managed a convincing laugh. "Neither do I. There is always a certain emotional adjustment to be made to a new roommate or housemate. And when I leave here, girl, I'm in no adjusting mood. Let's let it ride awhile, shall we? That motel I looked at takes steady tenants — "

Elsa jumped. The intercom had blared, "Hoyt — ten. Immediately."

"See you," she told Mitzi, and raced off, blessing the intercom or whoever had inspired the call. She found no emergency of any kind within her domain. Well, nice to know someone was keeping a protective eye upon her.

Yet if she gauged Mitzi correctly, she would not give up without extreme unpleasantness. Did Elsa want that with a nurse who could have worn a bikini on duty, she had such an in at Port Haven Hospital.

Oh, why had she listened to Crissman, then succumbed to the lure of steady duty? She knew why, of course, but she didn't know how she could help anyone. Or did she?

One thing her mother had drilled into Elsa was thought control. One couldn't be a dedicated nurse if the mind slipped constantly to personal matters. One

146

concentrated upon the subject at hand.

Wearily Elsa drove home, concentrating on her day off duty. Dinner. Roast beef and Yorkshire pudding. Oh, yes, baked lettuce. Did she remember how, or should she settle for chopped slaw with vinegary dressing? Dessert, hmmm. Seed cake? Well, hardly; she hadn't seen a caraway seed for years.

Oh, well, men always liked pie. And there were two men to consider.

Suppose Mitzi barged in, how would she handle her? Onto a pad went 'gate padlock' and then 'cardboard for sign; "DO NOT DISTURB AND I DO MEAN YOU."' And if she wanted to make anything of that, let her.

Why did life have to be so complicated? Why did so many feel they knew so much more about running your life than you could when basically their motives, clothed in 'good works,' were selfish?

So I tune out, Elsa informed herself that Tuesday noon, lifting the roast from the marinating bath that would promise meat as tender as her Dad — correction, Dr. Hoag — enjoyed.

Funny how she thought anything Dr.

Hoag would enjoy Dr. Steffner would enjoy because his chief did. That was devotion. She liked it.

The two men arrived. Steffner donned a work smock and bent to his chore. First he put the padlock on the garden gate, muttering, "The high cost of privacy." But he laughed as he muttered, and Elsa felt he approved.

"Oh, go stretch down." he snapped a bit at his chief, they being off duty, and like a cowed child, overdoing it a bit, Dr. Hoag stretched out in a chair, sighed deeply and to Elsa's, if not Steffner's amazement, promptly went to sleep.

"I don't understand how he stands up to — " He broke off.

"May I know what and why?" Elsa asked.

Steffner turned to look at her a moment, then shook his head. "The less you know, the better for you. At that, who does know anything? If Hoag did, he could fight. Those after him play behind his back. A less dedicated man would have given up three years ago."

Three years ago. Hmm. Well if she could pinpoint anything startling happening in that era, she might have some idea what had precipitated this situation.

"What are you doing, nurse? That tea — "

"Looks like coffee? Nicest compliment I ever had came from a British journalist. I thought I'd done rather well as a nurse, though he called me Sister. That he ignored. But when I took him a tray with a heated teapot and brewed him a *cuppa*, he said now he could live. He'd found someone who could hand him something other than colored water."

Steffner frowned, then smiled. Elsa had a second teapot ready. "For the not yet indoctrinated," she intoned. "Do bring him in to carve."

Dr. Hoag came in, took time to splash cold water on his face, then, looking more refreshed than Elsa had ever seen him, picked up fork and carving knife. Deftly he slashed, and thin slices fell in orderly fashion.

"Steffner, if I overeat?"

They carried trays to the garden, which would have been dark had not a teenage moon peered down and a single pole

149

lamp not shed a certain glow. Even the mosquitoes had given up and gone to other gardens.

"Ah," Dr. Hoag tried the Yorkshire pudding and beamed at Elsa, "does Mrs. Hoyt still make this on occasion?"

"No, she makes nothing of any kind. She is too busy to have a personal life. I don't know how she would have survived in pre-freezer days, unless, of course, she had every meal at the training school."

Later, much later, after an amazing amount of food had been consumed, Hoag asked idly if Elsa had any late photographs of her mother.

She brought some out, but it was Steffner who blurted, "Someone living behind an ever-closed door."

Elsa looked at him, startled. Could he read everyone that quickly? Why hadn't she seen that? She had often thought of her mother as one encased in a sense of duty. She, Elsa herself, seemed unable to reach through to her except professionally.

"Sorry," Steffner said.

"Oh, no," Elsa protested. "Rather, thank you. Now I can see that door."

Hoag had picked up two trays and taken them into the house, and Elsa had a moment alone with Steffner.

"You won't try to pry it open," he stated.

"What good would that do her? Or me?" she asked. "The person on the inside holds the key. Only she can open it, without destruction."

"For such a pretty girl — " the hazel brown eyes beamed at her — "you have a lot of intelligence."

And as they were off-duty, she answered him in kind. "And have you ever thought of indulging in psychomatic ophthalmology?"

"Now there's a six-bit word. Ah, so I look beyond the physical evidence. Will try."

Dr. Hoag had automatically picked up a tray and gone to the cottage. Steffner now followed, but he hurried back, smiling. "He's asleep again. These things can wait, can't they?"

"Of course," Elsa replied absently. "But why, if he can rest like this here, did he give up the cottage?"

"When he had it, he couldn't rest.

There would be someone pounding at the door or Conchita running loyal interference. Ah, I see you've had a taste. Then call it protocol rather than status."

He was ready to say more when there came a rustle of oleander branches. Elsa looked up and would have sworn the teenaged moon winked at her, then ducked its head.

"Continued in the next issue?" she whispered softly. "For even this hedge has ears." Then her voice rose. "I was interested in that little boy who darted across from the school bus and into the path of a truck that couldn't stop."

"Moral: even on highways stop if there's a school bus discharging. They are sometimes so little and so quick."

Yes, the lad would be all right, his lesson learned through pain. The truck driver had been ready to beat up those who wanted to pick up the boy; who thought it cruel to let him lie crumpled as they awaited the ambulance.

He then gave such a detailed account of the surgery necessary at the hospital, Elsa felt she was receiving first year anatomy, until she glanced at him and saw his eyes dancing.

"Oh," she said, knowing this was for the ears of the listener-in.

"Um," he replied, and she felt they'd established an all time high in communication.

She caught herself barely in time from asking about his brother. My, wouldn't the eavesdropper have made a mountain of that!

"Reminds me. Be right back; left something in the kitchen."

Steffner took off, but Elsa noticed he stopped first at the gate. Later, her ear's accustomed to sounds, she heard a car door close softly. Then he reappeared, a neat-sized box transistor with him.

"Patient mentioned a symphony on at nine. It's a little after. Ashkenazy and Barenboim with Mozart's Concerto in E Flat."

The music spread into the garden like a silver flood of moonlight. Steffner turned it down only a little, then, under its cover, they were free to talk a little.

"Familiar car east, parked," he told Elsa. "Probably calling on your neighbor." He looked up. "And not a chance of rain to drive them inside. Oh, well, you're refreshing even to remain silent around."

Refreshing? She felt anything but refreshed; rather, burdened with a new duty that seemed too heavy to carry. Couldn't he sense that? He could and made a tentative query.

"The why of it," she murmured; "the question of whether it is worth the destruction of his health. He could use that talent elsewhere." Her eyes said, "And so could you."

"Something about a challenge," he murmured. "Run out on it, and one of two things happens. Either you carry defeat into your profession, or you're faced with the same set of circumstances again and, having been beaten once — " He turned his hands upward to indicate the second round of the challenge could be twice as difficult.

"Does he think he can out-sit them? Does he see them, whoever they are, giving up? And aren't they gaining steadily, or are they?"

"I hope they are. Oh, now wait," as she bristled. "The sooner they come out in the open, and if their assurance builds up, they will — " The music stopped suddenly, and so did he.

"It's pretty fine for you stay on." His voice was a mere whisper. "It gives him faith, confidence — "

Dr. Hoag appeared in the doorway at that moment, stretching, yawning, and would have spoken. But both sprang up, fingers to lips, indicating the oleander hedge. Then they hurried into the cottage.

"Daughter," Hoag said, using the term deliberately, "this has been the most delightful and restful evening I've had in years. I am heading down to board The Moppet and pray I can remain awake until I hit the bunk."

Elsa stared at him. He'd even named his escape route for her. Hadn't he called her the moppet a thousand times when she was little and forever getting into trouble?

"Then wait another moment." Swiftly she encased the remaining roast and Yorkshire pudding and the one segment of pie left. "If you're taking tomorrow off, perhaps you can use these. I couldn't possibly eat my way through them."

As he carried the roaster to the car, Steffner said, "Don't do it. No, not the roast; don't entice him back. You'd either be identified or crucified, and what good would that do anyone?"

Dr. Hoag returned, caught Elsa by the elbows and bestowed a kiss on her brow. "You are a blessing," he said.

"One always follows the Chief, eh?" Steffner asked, took Elsa by the elbows and followed suit but with considerably more warmth. Then both men left.

Elsa stumbled back to the garden, sank into a chair and stared blindly at the transistor, now switched to modern music.

'Identified or crucified.' As though she cared. But she did care deeply about the effect of either on Hoag and Port Haven Hospital.

'The Great Scheme,' Mrs. Bains had called this undercover plan of Mitzi's. Mitzi and how many more, and who were they and, above all, why?

Would she tell if Elsa were to write and ask her? Could she, with her husband obviously involved and through him not merely her alimony but the care of her children. Above all, did she really know?

Elsa glanced at the sky, symbolic of an appeal for help. The stars seemed lower here than in Chicago. Perchance they were, as this was nearer the equator. Or was it the atmosphere? These seemed swung from the firmament on long chains. And she wished she were right up there on that wide, glistening one, far from what she faced.

She couldn't run away now, not after what Steffner had indicated. Yet now, more then ever, she needed to flee from Port Haven.

I, she informed herself, am deeply in love with Dr. Albert Steffner. I think I have been since I was fourteen, at least in love with the image he cast then. That's why I could not marry Bob immediately. And now I can never marry him.

"Well, if you ask me," came a strident voice next door, "second choice's better than none."

Bob, second choice, better than none? Steffner was the none.

It wasn't true, or fair to the 'second best'. Steffner had been like the sun hidden behind thick clouds. She hadn't identified him, only known he was there, someone who could so fill her life there could be room for no one else.

Now that he had emerged from behind the clouds of distance, she knew, and the knowledge was heartbreaking. He, so dedicated to her own former stepfather, who would believe Hoag had suffered from her own mother's actions and would view her from that vantage point and discard any growing emotional attachment to her.

I have to get away from here, she thought, turned off, then picked up his transistor and headed for the cottage. There is no sense in massaging an open wound.

First she had to write Bob. She did, quickly, decisively wondering, even as she wrote, if he wouldn't be relieved; if he perchance had not seen her as her mother's daughter, precise, definite, devoted only to her profession, qualities which would make her the ideal co-worker, i.e. wife? Hadn't that always been the barrier between them?

The letter written, she drove to town to mail it lest she weaken before dawn, then idled her way back, watching the glowing white curves of surf, a flounce below the avenue.

She would leave as soon as Port Haven could find a replacement, or summer vacations were over. They were nearing an end.

'Leave this problem unsolved?' jeered an inner voice.

'Well, if those on the inside can't solve it, for goodness sake, what chance have I?'

Back came the challenge. 'Decisions should be viewed from all angles, given deep thought, evaluation. Hasty action can bring chaos.'

There was a car in front of her house. On the tiny veranda sat Mitzi.

"Woman without a home," she informed Elsa. "Could you put me up for the night at least?"

Could she? Why not? Why not take the enemy into her camp? What quicker way could there be to learn the basis of The Great Scheme?

"Or were you — " Mitzi smirked, and Elsa clenched a fist — "expecting some of your company to return?"

10

ELSA curbed the desire to ask Mitzi if her company were inclined to return later. Instead she smiled and said she was not expecting anyone. The locks had been replaced and, as a thank-you, she had prepared dinner for them. Just a light repast. No, she doubted there was anything edible left. She hoped not. She grew so tired of leftovers.

She conducted Mitzi to the front bedroom and was rewarded with, "I should think you'd prefer this to that back room."

"I would if newsboys didn't come equipped with Hondas. Believe me, here you can identify each stop the morning paper boy makes. After a rough night — "

Nurses, Elsa thought, were trained to give the 'reply diplomatic.' Something told her that training was going to be tested to its utmost with this young woman around. For here came the swift counter-challenge.

"And you from — you did say Chicago, didn't you? Are the nights there so quiet?"

"Peculiar, isn't it? One's hearing becomes so adjusted to a steady roar it is no more than background. But in the silence, a break by a sharp noise can be shattering."

"I suppose," Mitzi murmured.

"Then you are not from a city of any size?" Just what was this other girl's background? She had never heard even an inkling from anyone.

There was a moment's hesitation; then Mitzi murmured, through yawns, that she had trained in "Shrevepo't," and Elsa made the leap to northern Louisanna. No further. Her guest was 'beat'. If Hoyt didn't mind, she'd retire immediately.

Carefully Elsa retreated, carrying a thought with her as though it were a precious gem. The way to stop Mitzi from questioning was to counter-question swiftly.

She herself did not sleep too well. When she could bring her mind-versus-heart down out of the clouds where the love she felt for Steffner had to remain, she went back over the evening, the quiet joy of it despite the insidious interruptions from the next garden.

What would Drs. Hoag and Steffner think if they knew she was housing Mitzi? Steffner would know it had been planned. He had recognized her car but hadn't identified it to Elsa.

And what of the morrow? Could she, did she want to rid herself of Mitzi before she had had a chance to squeeze information from her as she obviously did from others?

A breeze sprang up and clinked the blinds. Irritably Elsa sat up and pulled them to a solid high. The garden. Mrs. Misinformation. She was as much a part of the garden as the palm tree that stood now like an upended powder puff.

Ah, but she had recognized the neighbor as a threat. Well, good. A battle was half won if the enemy were identified and his methods of warfare known in advance. She knew a few of Mitzi's.

Next she had to consider the cost of the risk. Let that person once suspect she was in the other camp and she, Elsa, doubted Mitzi would stop at anything to disqualify her. Was this worth it?

Elsa had a sudden memory of a patient who, faced with veritable dissolution of her worldly goods, had said, 'It is one's purported friends who are the greatest danger. Inspired, they would say, by good works or intensions, they can wreak havoc faster than any enemy against whom we're braced.'

Fortified by this memory, Elsa slept. With no illusions about Mitzi, she had a fighting chance to win.

She slept late. When she awakened, she looked out to see Mitzi in a bikini, sun-baking. Her off duty day? Or was she now on the four-to-midnight shift?

Mitzi saw her and was up immediately. "I've had my breakfast," she caroled, much to loudly. "Slip into something, and I'll serve you yours out here."

The oleanders flapped their green ears, and Elsa saluted them and their now blazing blossoms.

"With my northern hide?" she returned. "No, thank you."

"Oh, I'll find you a shady spot."

"Mitzi, I know what is good for me. You don't. Right?"

Now she knew the meaning of an 'anxious stomach,' Elsa thought. Mitzi was up to something or she would not want an eavesdropper to act as witness. And Elsa wanted no food.

And here it came. Laughing, the other entered. "Little Jed Bain told me you were really cooked that first day at the beach. Nice of you to have the children up for a cookout; they had such a good time. What did you think of their mother?"

"I have learned not to judge a person by a chance meeting."

"Oh, but you must have had some impression."

"The only impression I had at that time was of sun on skin. Isn't it strange more people don't recognize the danger of sunburn?"

Mitzi's mouth quirked and words began to form, but Elsa was there first.

"I remember one patient who'd flown south, baked, was flown back and nearly died. Dehydrated. Dr. Larkin tried to explain to her that it wasn't what burned one, but how deeply one was burned." And she went on didactically until Mitzi's face revealed she had given up temporarily.

"We have them often in Port Haven. What do you think of our hospital in comparison to those in which you served up north?"

"Actually, I haven't given it much thought one way or another. I am here on such a temporary basis. There does seem to be some inter-staff disagreement. I presume that is true everywhere and only shows up with the nurses in a smaller spot."

"You are naïve," murmured Mitzi, and served Elsa coffee which, to her northern taste, seemed more like mud in taste and texture.

"Sorry," Elsa muttered. "I'll whisk up some instant. This takes getting accustomed to. So I'm naïve? What is wrong at Port Haven or is it important that I know?" Elsa spoke over her shoulder as she filled a small teakettle and set it on a hot plate, wondering if Mitzi was aware of the liberties she had taken in another's home.

"As a dedicated nurse, you should know, certainly. It's a modern hospital with a horse-and-buggy man at the reins. Honestly, Hoyt, Port Haven could be coining money to turn back into equipment, but does it? Well, hardly.

"Take the Medicare patients. He lets them slip right through our fingers."

"Oh? How does one do that?"

"He doesn't hospitalize unless — well, unless the patient is in desperate need. Then after discharge, does he keep them coming back as outpatients? No."

Elsa nodded. Dr. Hoag would know their financial background. He would weigh the strain of their meeting their percentage of Medicare benefits against their actual need and act accordingly. She doubted any were discharged unless their convalescence records so indicated.

"Actually," Mitzi made this a final pronouncement, "he has about as much business acumen as a nurse's aide."

Elsa turned with her freshly made coffee and, seeing Mitzi's stare, shrugged her shoulders. "All of which is none of my business," she said. "Oh, thank you for the fresh toast. I do like it crisp."

"Just don't enjoy it too much. Ruark said he might drop in for lunch." Then quickly she covered her assumption of the role of hostess in the home of a comparative stranger. "He has a house call on a patient down the street."

Steadily Elsa looked at the toast. So it had been Ruark who had given the neighbor those pills little Dodie had ingested.

And now how to get rid of this menace?

How, for goodness sake, had Mitzi contacted Ruark? The telephone was still beside Elsa's bed. She was too well trained as a nurse to have anyone call in such close proximity. It meant only one thing. Mitzi had planned this in advance, well in advance, probably the night she had overheard Dr. Hoag arrange to change locks.

She wondered how her mother would have handled such a situation, then knew no such situation could have involved her. Mrs. Hoyt had that air of supremacy which would have made even Mitzi recoil.

And how would she have handled

her on the hospital staff? She wouldn't. Mitzi would have been bounced off, unless —

It was that *unless* that stopped Elsa from a normal reaction to such a take-over. Well, she need not remain to be further insulted, and once the breakfast dishes were left to drain (Mitzi had other things to do), she dressed, went to her car, returned and asked her unbidden guest to remove hers so Elsa might drive out.

"I wouldn't think of intruding on your little luncheon with Dr. Ruark," Elsa returned Mitzi's invitation she stay. "Frankly, Duval, I wasn't reared to intrude. 'Bye now."

Where did one go at a time like this without danger of being followed? Elsa went first to a stationery store, then equipped with paper and auxiliary pen and envelopes, headed across to the mainland.

It was good to have a mother one could talk to with the assurance of being understood. And she was, she knew from Mrs. Hoyt's replies to her earlier letters.

'I had no valid excuse to turn her away last night. There's a convention on, and I know every motel and hotel is crammed even on the mainland. So we ask why she didn't appeal to some old friend or acquaintance and then ask if she has any who would give her house room. She would know that. Besides, she was determined to worm her way in here. She has. To force her out would cause her to blame Dr. Hoag; making something of it that would recoil on him. I refuse her that power.'

Only those who had known Elsa over a period of time could evaluate her personality. She did not indulge in verbal brawls. To those questioning this, she would reply, "What is the percentage? I refuse to be anyone's bunching ball."

To one of Mitzi's caliber, Elsa was a toy doll who could be moved around at her, Mitzi's will. She had managed to get into the house, hadn't she? Well, just let that little softy try to put her out. Not that she would; she hadn't the gumption.

169

"What's Hoag going to say when he hears you're here?" Ruark asked.

"Just let him try to budge me," Mitzi threatened. "I'll go right to the powers that be, and he'll be sat back where he belongs."

"Use discretion, girl. Savorn can be pushed too far, you know. Too far means back over the line to the order side."

Elsa was also wondering what Dr. Hoag would say and trying to work out some means of alerting him to her intensions. She tore up many sheets before she wrote what she believed was comprehensible.

'I once heard you say one could not make an accurate diagnosis without complete examination and tests. I found a certain sickness within an establishment. I have been given the opportunity to run the tests. Believe in me. Trust me.' She signed it: 'Moppet.'

Now to alert Conchita. She could deliver the note with a privacy Elsa couldn't achieve, not knowing which members of the hospital staff were pro and which con Hoag.

Driving down the old road, Elsa marveled that so many houses of her earlier era still stood. She shuddered when she came to Conchita's village. She had thought this type long out of existence, but there they stood, wooden flats reared high on tall wooden legs.

Conchita was instantly alert. *Si*, she would be silent around the woman who came to stay. And *si*, she would slip to the doctair the note with not a one knowing. She would have — she patted her plump stomach — "the pain here."

"You are not afraid I'll fail?" Elsa remarked.

She wasn't. "You fight with the fist, you get the beating. I know you. You fight with the brain; she no know you have one. You win."

Elsa refused lunch, saying it was better she not be seen there, to tell anyone asking she had come down to 'pay' for some ironing she had brought along.

There remained now only the one, the most personal and the most heartbreaking aspect of her decision to face. There was nothing she could do about it. Dr. Steffner would simply have to judge her from his own point of view. To have him show any belief in her could raze the structure of the plan slowly forming in her mind.

One blessing: she was on midnight to dawn duty. He was rarely around Port Haven Hospital at that time.

That duty was a mixed blessing. Heat records were being broken. Duty after midnight in an air-conditioned atmosphere was a relief. Trying to rest during the heat-ridden hours, was agony to one unaccustomed to such heat and humidity.

Elsa felt she was suspended over a volcano which might erupt at any time. Mitzi was demanding her acceptance as a co-renter of the cottage so she might take her personal belongings out of storage. And Elsa was holding out pending word from her vacationing friend.

She had had one brief word with Dr. Hoag, who had chanced to be leaving the hospital after a late call. He had said, frowning, "Good girl, but watch it. Dynamite. Yet somehow I'm counting on you winning." And he walked off, leaving her still staring at a case history on her clip board.

Steffner, in their encounter, had said nothing. He hadn't needed words. Elsa had received from him a look of utter contempt.

She supposed that was good. Surely had he had even a touch of the devotion she felt toward him, he would have sensed her motivation, had confidence in her handling of the situation.

"He only bites on Sundays," a voice behind her commented softly. Turning, she found Ruark there. "Speaking of Sundays, why don't we give that garden of yours a real initiation, have a group of friendly souls in after sundown?"

Elsa hesitated only a moment. What quicker way to identify the enemies?

"I suppose." She hesitated, then added the word, "Time."

"Oh, that. Duval is taking the full weekend off. She can do the heavy work; you'll only have to bow in as hostess."

Elsa went frowning on her way, stopping first at the post office.

A letter from Bob. His reply to her

announcement she was breaking their engagement.

She sat for a long time in her car, fingering the envelope. It was not thick, but then Bob was incapable of writing more than pertinent findings.

His words left her gasping. The opening line was, 'For the first time I am confident our marriage would be a success. Emotions, even as blood samples, should be given a test run. You've been in that tube but haven't read your findings correctly. I'll be down to handle that delicate evaluation, having had a bit more experience than you.'

Elsa's head went down on the car steering wheel. Having Bob around at a time like this was all she needed to induce a complete crack-up. She feared now that she had made the wrong decision at every turn of the road and faced only confusion, a veritable emotional melee which could ruin more than it helped.

A drive-in and a tasteless lunch, and Elsa thought even as she, a nurse, depended upon physicians with their greater knowledge for any decisive action, so she should have withdrawn and let some other person with the same talent direct her.

It was too late now. When she reached the cottage, she found Mitzi absent but her personal gear all over the place. Inwardly she raged at the presumption, then turned her rage back upon herself. She had allowed this to happen, and for a purpose.

Dinner she overlooked. Then, dressing for the hospital, she found her lips curved in a most peculiar fashion. Wise Mitzi was not risking an immediate personal contact. She would wait for Elsa to 'turn off.'

And then the nurse in Elsa forgot Mitzi, the problem her presence posed. She was placed on duty in the intensive care ward, her first patient a tiny child suffering from 'crib sickness,' a new and dangerous virus which was striking babies from every type of home.

What were her personal problems compared with the grief and anxiety of the baby's parents? Under Dr. Bain's steady encouragement, Elsa worked with the child, watched and, at dawn, relaxed.

"What do you think of Mitzi?" Bain

asked as they went down for coffee, the crisis passed.

"Mitzi?" Elsa asked vaguely. "Well, really I've hardly seen her. She's at the cottage only temporarily, you know."

"Oh?" And the subject was dropped.

Mitzi was awaiting her on her return at dawn, yawning a little but looking delectable in a flowered housecoat.

"Darling, I've a proposition to put to you. This place, this crazy little cottage, I love. I have to have it. Now you talk old Hoag into selling it to you. I'll put up the money, cold cash; then you in turn sell it to me. Is it a deal?"

Swiftly Elsa reached for caution, for wisdom, for all of the attributes she was going to need to meet this crisis.

"What makes you think he'd sell to me?" she managed.

"He's gone for broke, both he and his interest in the hospital. He'll grab any cold cash for a getaway."

11

ELSA'S complete shock and bewilderment was so obvious she did not have to act. And Mitzi recognized the authenticity of her shock.

"But, Hoyt, it was bound to happen. Of course you don't know the background, his utterly inane ideas and the men he talked into backing him financially. Well, they're tired of it; they're going to foreclose on him any day now."

"Then wouldn't he want this as a — well, a retreat?"

"Are you crazy? Stay here in this city after such a flop? He does have that boat, you know. He'll use that to make a fast getaway before that too is — "

"That too? Then why not this?"

"If we act fast we can get clear title, and he'll have a few dollars to see him to his next port of call. Agreed?"

What should she say or do? If Mitzi was right, Dr. Hoag would welcome the extra money. And something told Elsa

177

she was right at least in her financial evaluation.

"Talk to me later," she pleaded. "I'm too tired to think. We had a crib-fever emergency."

"Oh, well, if you insist, though I think — I mean I can use these morning hours to get things under way."

Elsa stood up and now her voice was firm. "I have no intention of doing anything, feeling as exhausted as I do. I owe it to my profession to take some rest immediately. I'll talk to you after that, say at one o'clock."

She wrestled with the decision as she sought to sleep. If Mitzi were telling the truth, she would purchase the cottage and then keep it. But could she? Had she enough money saved, or had her mother loaned her enough to see her through?

Above all, if she did make the purchase, then refused to sell to Mitzi, could she remain on at Port Haven Hospital, assured of the income which would make continuing to live there possible? And why should she? She really belonged in Chicago. Well, didn't she? Steffner? Ha!

Eventually she slept and had a nightmare in which she found herself being shoved first one way, then another, then whirled around until she awakened to find herself hanging to the edge of the bed in vertigo.

In another moment she had the perfect answer, and when she awakened at noon to find Mitzi standing over her with coffee, made as Elsa preferred, she was ready with it.

"Ready to talk business?" Mitzi asked a little later.

"Not until I've talked it over with my mother," Elsa returned.

"Are you out of your mind?" cried Mitzi. "Your mother is in Chicago, and we have to work fast."

"Ummm. Well, one of my closest friends is a newspaper reporter; covers courts. I know, through him, how fast these fast deals boomerang. You might have the purest of intentions, but I might be the one to get stuck with something that hadn't a clear title, and you wouldn't touch me with a ten-foot pole when you found out."

"Call her," snapped Mitzi.

"At this hour? Now who's out of her mind? In what kind of a hospital did you train? Could your dean take time off at midday to consider a real estate deal?"

And then her delayed action temper took over. "Look, Mitzi, if you don't approve of the way I run my life, you know what to do. Get out. You'll find something as soon as this convention is over."

"Oh, calm down. You did have a tough night, didn't you? I was only trying to help old Hoag out of a bind."

"Maybe if you told me something about that bind, I'd feel better about going through with the deal," Elsa murmured.

She sat, blonde curls rumpled from her restless night, face drained of color, looking, Mitzi thought, like an addlepated infant.

"Give me your word you won't broadcast a line of what I tell you?"

Large grey-blue eyes lifted to Mitzi, and solemnly Elsa took the oath. She wouldn't. But just having this information herself could help immeasurably, she thought.

"All right; settle back while I brief you."

Half an hour later Elsa was still sitting in bed, back propped by pillows but so soul-sick she felt a deep need of something to prop her spirits. So this was the Great Scheme Della Bain had mentioned. A complete take-over of Port Haven Hospital by the anti-Hoags; the hospital then would be run as a business enterprise, 'a real money-maker.'

Nor could she, Elsa, see any way to save Dr. Hoag or save the hospital from these opportunists. No wonder he looked so whipped. But what stubbornness or dedication. What kept him fighting on instead of going elsewhere? There were other patients in other cities.

And Steffner, too, was staying on, fighting with Hoag. He was too young to give up his future lest there be some way out.

But oh, the strain under which they worked. Especially Hoag, his antennas ever out to sense some violation of his brand of ethics. Such as the diet pills? He'd slipped up there. Or had he? Those had been delivered not from the hospital or by prescription, but by hand. She could prove that.

Perhaps it was right that she, Elsa, had been there at the cottage, had known what to do and that Dr. Hoag had been available to confirm the emetic she had given. Or another black mark could have been placed against Port Haven Hospital.

"Well," Mitzi came in brightly, "now what do you think?"

Swiftly Elsa supplied that ingredient. "Why stay on here and get mixed up in such a miserable situation? My rent is up next week. I'm pulling out, going back to where physicians and nurses consider the patients first; cold cash, second. You'd better start looking for lodging."

"Of all the ingrates! I suppose you'll broadcast what I said — "

"Do *you*? When you've given oath?" Elsa asked innocently.

"Well, do get out of this room. I swear the skies are loaded with lead. Looks like sun, but it is heavy. The living room is bearable. A better ventilating system should be put in. I've checked with Harbor Electric; they'll move when I give the word."

"Then hold it. I'm about fed up with this heat. Hurricane build-up. At least that's what some newscaster said last night."

"Where are you going now?"

"As you know, I did not come prepared to stay. I brought no off-duty clothes. I'd like to look like something other than a nurse at your garden party tomorrow night."

"I'll go with you."

"Good." Elsa hid her smile. Mitzi was now afraid to let her out of her sight. "Just don't try to make me purchase a dress I can't wear properly bending over."

"Oh, I'll drop for groceries while you shop for glamour."

"Glamour? Me?" But her ready acquiescence threw Mitzi off guard.

Elsa did not know why she chose that particular frock at that particular time. Later she could cast back and pinpoint the reflex, but in the smart shop to which Mitzi conducted her she made her purchase despite her companions. "Well, really, Hoyt — "

"I like it."

"But it's — well, infantile," cried Mitzi.

Perhaps. Squared neck with a white ruffle, blue-striped, tent contoured, another ruffle flouncing the hem line. And childish slippers to match.

Nor did Mitzi shop for groceries until she was confident Elsa would remain in a shady spot in her, Mitzi's car.

Interesting, thought Elsa, or could be if so many lives were not involved. I do wonder what she did to put Salvorn under her thumb as she has; Salvorn, a multi millionaire who still lived in the many-domed mansion his grandfather had built many years ago.

It was puzzling. Mitzi was capable of being paid off, accepting money for silence, yet this obviously hadn't been suggested. Mitzi was fishing for larger, more enduring benefits. Port Haven Hospital and Bain, (who would by then be free to marry her) as chief of staff, Ruark a medical crown prince.

Ruark. Something told Elsa she could win him quickly if he was convinced she would swing to their side. As though any man were worth going against one's deepest convictions. Steffner? Ah, but he wouldn't be the Steffner she loved if he had that quality.

As Elsa approached Port Haven Hospital that night, she saw it in a new perspective, not the strongly built haven for the sick in body and at times, mind, but a fragile, beautiful tier of floors stretching to the hot, dark blue sky on unsteady financial pinions.

It wasn't a quiet night. Even in the cooled air-conditioned interior, some of the heaviness of the out-of-doors seemed to seep in. Temperatures flared, anxieties erupted as suppuration in hitherto quiet skin areas; children were fretful, adults restless. In one ward definite fear lay like a pall.

Someone had had his transistor on. Hurricane Hannah could be heading their way. And they were bed-bound. What would they, could they do if it struck there?

"Hannah," Elsa returned. "Say your alphabet over. The H means seven have headed this way. Now why should the H, the eighth, strike here?"

Well, this year had been different;

records had been broken all over the nation.

One elderly man remembered the Great Blow that had struck this very island fifty years ago. Didn't have the warning systems they had these days: nothing but telegraph. Weather folk turned on a red light top of the courthouse as a warning, but few paid it any mind.

He talked. He told in great detail what he'd seen, what his friends had seen, the experiences of others he'd heard about, the devastation. And Elsa let him talk. Soon patients were yawning, sliding down in their beds, sleeping.

Yet she found this the most difficult night she had spent at the hospital. Where before she had known there were dissenters, she hadn't known of their power. Now she looked at each nurse, orderly, physician as though to probe to his or her feeling toward the hospital, its staff, their relationship.

Would they swing to the new directors easily or, driven by financial or professional need, accept their dictation?

Providing, of course, there was a change. Yet Mitzi had seemed positive, and from what she had said, Elsa had few doubts.

"You look tired," Rawlings, coming on duty early, told Elsa.

"Weather," Elsa evaded the true issue. "It does drain a newcomer of energy."

"Getting adequate rest with your house guest around?"

"I doubt I will today. She and her cohorts — that is, sorry, friends — are planning a yard party at sundown."

"Well, if you need rest, run over to my place. The men aren't working today. And they're nearly through. I slept yesterday without leaping into the air once."

But driving back to the cottage, Elsa admitted to herself that her weariness and inner sickness came from what Mitzi had revealed.

She left her car in a parking area some distance from the cottage for two reasons. She wanted it free for quick flight should she need it, and she wanted, if possible, to slip into the cottage and gain such rest as she could before the activity started.

So drained of energy was she that Mitzi, sleeping with one ear open for her return, didn't hear her enter. And when she finally decided to check, Elsa was deeply asleep.

At some period, late in the morning, an uneasiness disturbed Elsa's slumber. Not actual noise, but a queer feeling. As though I were in the eye of a hurricane, she thought. For wasn't that spot supposed to be without activity while around it roiled and boiled the massive build-up of fury?

A glance out of the window, and she saw long tables had been brought in to form a massive U. Groups of chairs and small tables dotted the lawn, a focus for tray-bearing guests after they had idled along the buffet.

Beyond her door were low voices interspersed with, "shhh, you'll waken her."

As the garden party wasn't to start until nearly sundown, this could go on all day. Elsa wished she had an escape hatch, or even a bolt to her door.

Now she sympathized with patients no longer in pain yet who had to lie awaiting discharge. Frustrating. Or was it?

Low voices outside of her window.

"I don't know," a man was saying. "Something the Mitz hatched up for some reason, as though she was ready for us to show our colors, our strength."

"Mobilization," agreed the other. "But I wish she'd picked a cooler day. What's the latest on Hannah?"

"Not good. Heading for the coast curve, but who knows where? I remember times we battened down only to have a wind-witch suddenly switch and bypass us fifty miles down the Gulf."

"Any time element offered?"

"Think the last was ten hours, but that was a few hours ago. Where's your transistor?"

Elsa became alert. Her car was in a wide open space. She might need it. Now where could she park with any assurance she could get out and on to the hospital if called after heavy winds started?

Suddenly she thought of Conchita in her high-raised cottage. One blast could level that. Ramondo had a truck. He was about to have a car as well, with the understanding he would come after her if the storm headed in.

And this gave her a good excuse to be

absent from the cottage until the party started.

How do I get into these situations? she thought, rerunning her old record. Here she stood, pressed back in a corner of her own kitchen to keep out from the swift passage of nurses and aides in mufti, rapidly preparing food. Her food was coffee and a sleazy piece of toast.

Mitzi came in from the garden, face flushed, brow beaded. "Elsa," she cried, "why don't you go to your room? You need rest."

"In there?" Elsa retorted idly. "Besides, I have an errand at the Rodriquezes'. I'll spin down and be back in no time."

She found the Mexican family busily packing the truck with personal belongings. They were excited. They had been warned by their priest at early mass. All families in this area were to move to the recreation hall which stood in the lee of the great stone cathedral.

The car they could use to pick up elderly people, Ramondo assured her, beaming. And should the report come that the storm, Hannah, strike there soon, he would come for the *señorita* and go to the hospital.

She was to go home now; in maybe an hour he would come for the car. A friend would drive his truck.

An hour. Perversely Elsa, now hungry, drove southwest to a small café, picked up a sandwich and a carton of coffee and went onto the low-lying end of the Island to sit and gaze out to the southwest.

At first glance it seemed no more than a murky band many sky-miles away; then little wisps licked at the top, stretched to streamers. She turned the car away from the menacing view, then braked.

It was right there she had first met Steffner those many years ago. But how the site had changed, even as he and she.

Unhappily she drove away, aware that behind her were low-lying sand dunes with cherished homes riding their crests. Perhaps the population explosion was responsible for realty promoters building without thought of danger to the eventual residents.

Yet how could anyone determine potential danger? Hadn't newspapers carried the story of an old home which had stood staunchly in a quiet neighborhood for years; then whose occupants were killed by a crashing plane?

Elsa slid into the cottage almost unobserved. Mitzi and her friends were dressing, readying themselves for early guests.

Carelessly Elsa donned the new frock, brushed her curls back and stepped out to find a new Mitzi. She looked regal, gracious, older. Why? wondered Elsa.

Sheer black with a white trim and definitely midi-length, almost maxi. Her hair a polished black swirl, neither too high nor too low.

"Come on." She yanked at Elsa's arm a little. "The guest of honor is driving up. I had him come a little early. Car congestion," she explained.

They stood in the shadow of Junior, the stunted palm at the entrance to the garden. The tall man getting out of his car looked, then looked again, then strode forward.

In another moment Elsa found herself in his arms.

"Moppet," he cried, "you here? Mitzi,

is this the surprise? Why child," he looked down at Elsa, "you haven't grown an inch."

"Moppet?" Mitzi grabbed Elsa from his embrace, found someone else taking the guests's attention, and shook her. "You little idiot, why didn't you tell me you were Hoag's stepdaughter? We needn't have gone to this expense. But, girl, have we got him whipped now. Who's that?"

Elsa was shaking her head. This man she knew only as Sam. Sam what? She'd never known nor cared. He'd been one of Dr. Hoag's closest friends. Then suddenly she did know. He was the Salvorn who controlled the Port Haven Hospital finances, who held the liens on the place and intended foreclosing.

"Well, Elsie," his voice boomed again, "you too? This is old home week. Just met the Moppet."

"Mother — " Elsa's voice was unbelieving; then in still greater shock she cried, "Bob — " For beside Mrs. Hoyt stood the man she'd thought she had put out of her life forever.

12

EYE of the hurricane? But no, that was where the strength lay. She had none, and it seemed everyone nearby was staring at her, demanding something. What?

"I am very tired," Mrs. Hoyt broke the silence. "Elsa, if you will show me to my room — "

Elsa looked at Mitzi, then shrugged. Where could she send her unbidden guest at a time like this?

"And Bob," Mrs. Hoyt reminded her. "We flew down, you know, both after a rugged four-to-midnight."

Guests were coming in, cars easing into parking areas, guests easing through the garden gate, aware there was some crisis there under the stunted palm.

Elsa turned to Mitzi. "If you will clear your room and put your personal effects in your car, Mother can take that. Bob, I'd offer you mine, but it's like a furnace. I suggest the divan in the front room; the party noise shouldn't reach there."

"Party?" Mrs. Hoyt took the helm. "You mentioned none in your letters. A surprise for you?"

Mitzi stepped up to explain and found herself facing a Waterloo.

"And you a nurse," was Mrs. Hoyt's only comment.

"You are flying back tonight? Tomorrow?" Mitzi tried to reclaim her superiority.

"No," came the answer in a tone that marveled she should have asked. "I am here for a vacation. Now, Elsa, if you'll — "

Elsa was aware of Salvorn watching, a withdrawn, calculating look on now grim features. Once he stepped forward, and she felt he was about to offer the hospitality of his many-roomed home to her mother; then he eased back again.

Mitzi, aware of this, made another try at charming the new guest. "It is obvious your daughter did not tell you we were sharing quarters."

"Sharing?" Mrs. Hoyt's voice was crisp. "She mentioned some nurse coming at midnight and she giving her safe haven until she could find other quarters."

"Elsa — " Mitzi began a reproof, but Salvorn stepped in.

"I don't know about the rest of you," he began, "but I am slowly starving to death. May I suggest we all have a bite to eat? We may need our strength before morning if what that transistor has been forecasting comes to pass. Elsie?"

"Excellent idea," she agreed, and took his arm.

"Elsa?" And Elsa accepted Bob Latoret's arm, and stumbled a little at that as she walked the familiar path.

She looked back once. Mitzi stood with fury in her eyes. She had, Elsa deduced, planned on Salvorn as her prize of the evening. Instead she had been left alone, supposedly to clear her quarters for the incoming guest.

"Who is that chap?" Bob asked quietly.

"I know his name," Elsa parried, "and what he means to the island. But, Bob, I haven't seen him since he was the youngest son of a wealthy family, forever in trouble Dad was getting him out of. He's changed through the years. I'd never have recognized him."

Mitzi suddenly appeared, attempting to recapture her role as hostess of the evening. Voice a little strident, she introduced the guest who'd just flown down from Chicago.

"Mrs. Hoag, Dr. Hoag's ex-wife, y'know."

Elsa stiffened, awaiting her mother's rapid retort. But it didn't come. Instead, Elsie Hoyt smiled, said, "Charmed," then added, "I am dean of nurses at Northwestern. We do train our girls a bit differently from the way they do down here."

"Bob," Elsa whispered, "why did Mother come?"

"Your guess is as good as mine. She blamed the hurricane."

"And you?"

"How can I run a test with the specimen a thousand miles away?" And he smiled at a nurse nearby, who promptly gave up allegiance to the man to whom she was engaged. Imagine that foolish little Elsa being able to isolate a handsome creature like this black-haired, black-eyed man.

Salvorn managed to isolate Elsa between

the smoked oysters and the crab filet. "Your party?" he asked, and when she shook her head, "Nor do you approve. Do you know why?"

She looked up at him, her eyes wide. "Oh, yes. I had a decision to make. I made it. I am not sorry. But tell me, how did you recognize me? Surely in the many years that have passed I've changed. You have."

"How?"

"Matured mentally," she murmured.

"I wonder," he muttered, then turned to some one who had approached from the other side.

Latoret came up again, frowning. "Who's the chap who just came in? He asked for you, and that Mitzi said you were bespoken."

Elsa glanced over to see Ruark frowning at her, even as Mitzi sought to hold his attention and Dr. Bain, on the other side, to prod him on toward her.

Then suddenly she saw the picture in its entirety. Here in her garden were all of the principals in The Great Scheme, from Bain to the lowliest aide. And, she added, each was ready to speak a pre-rehearsed piece for the one who counted for them, Sam Salvorn. But what a meager crew had been left at the hospital.

Suddenly all were aware of some change in the atmosphere, as though a great sigh had swept in from the Gulf, bending the oleanders, rustling the palms.

A moment later an excited aide stepped to the rear door.

"All hands on deck," she caroled. "Port Haven just called. Everyone connected with the hospital is to report for duty immediately. Hannah is on her way in. She's centering on our island."

Elsa glanced first toward her mother. She was not a member of Port Haven's staff, yet she had literally bristled and now stood at what her daughter called 'attention.'

Beside her, Bob Latoret muttered, "I too can give a hand."

Dr. Ruark strode toward Elsa. "Some chap gave me the keys to your car. Come on; I'll run you in."

Automatically Elsa handed the keys to Latoret. "Will you see to Mother?" And then she paused.

Dr. Steffner was striding in, his gaze picking up, then discarding each person he found there until he centered on Elsa.

"You are needed at Port Haven. Pick up a uniform and make it snappy. Listen to that."

They all listened. That first sigh had grown in scope, in intensity. But sighs paused. This did not. This vast outpouring of wind was a steady, pressuring flow of air which sent those in the garden scurrying for their personal belongings, sent cars speeding along boulevards, heading toward Port Haven Hospital.

"Dr. Steffner, my mother — "

"Will I be of use?" Mrs. Hoyt asked.

For all of a moment Steffner hesitated; then he nodded. "Rawlings was caught in that first gust. We need someone to deploy nurses and aides for what lies ahead. Hoyt?"

"Yes, Dr. Steffner," she responded.

In another moment she had sped in, grabbed her ever-ready bag and was out and getting into his car.

"Why me especially?" she asked.

"Dr. Hoag wanted you at the hospital

where you would be safe and he would not have to worry."

Then why hadn't he telephoned? Why send this particular man who was so greatly needed in an emergency? And would she be safe at the hospital, which reared into the air while the little tan cottage cowered above flood tide lines, offering little resistance to wind.

It didn't make sense. Nothing did. Steffner's heavy car was being buffeted until Elsa had to hang on to maintain her balance.

And there, ahead — what had happened to Port Haven Hospital?

She voiced the question, and Steffner snapped the answer.

"You do not see glass windows because storm protectors have been dropped over them. You will find many changes within, all manipulated instantly to make of this place a true haven.

"And this protection is what has thrown Hoag to the wolves. First your mother, as you know, fought his investment. She didn't stay to see it through. Salvorn picked up when finances ran low. And he too thought Hoag a visionary, the vision a fool nightmare."

"But I didn't know about mother's decision. I'd been sent away to boarding school. I've never known. I only knew Duval was brewing up something and felt I had to find out so I might help Dad."

They had wheeled into the shelter of the lea side of the hospital. Steffner had time only to pat her, say, "Good girl," then leap out in response to the intercom.

Hurricanes, Elsa was to learn, presented many facets. To those at Port Haven Hospital they brought human wreckage; some were injured even as they sought to bring others in for help.

Outside, there was the steady roar of ever mounting wind; inside, a peculiar silence, as each staff member was intent upon his duty, unaware of self.

Once a mighty bang sounded, and someone reported a metal roof had been lifted from a building far away and carried aloft until the hospital's southwestern wall offered an impediment.

Port Haven Hospital had its own auxiliary motor plant to supply electric power. It had its 'Hoag's Folly,' a mighty tank with water kept fresh until, at a time like this, the supply was swiftly cut off lest it be contaminated.

"In the old days," Bob looked up from a child's arm, "the Indians dipped their arrows in poison. We use rusty metal."

"How many anti-tetanus shots have you given?" murmured Elsa.

"Lost count. Next. Oh, Elsa, take her to some place they call 'letdown.' A lot of youngsters are sitting it out."

Letdown was the relaxation suite to the northeast where, if there ever was time, nurses eased in on comfortable lounging chairs for a moment's rest.

The big rooms seemed filled with children and, to Elsa's amazement, was presided over by a corps of teenage girls who had the youngsters' attention distracted from the storm with games.

A lovely dark-eyed sixteen-year-old came up for the child Elsa was now carrying.

"I'll take her," the girl said. Then brightly, "oh, you're the one Dad called the moppet, aren't you? Mitzi has told us a lot about you."

"Mitzi?" puzzled Elsa.

"She saved my life, you know. I fell overboard in shark-infested water. She was on another craft. She didn't wait for anything; she just dove in and began towing me to her boat. At that, she got nipped on the heel by a shark before someone threw a harpoon."

Elsa went back to her post in a daze. Mitzi would have done exactly that, without thought about whom she was saving, without thought of the consequences.

No wonder Salvorn had listened to her evaluation of Dr. Hoag.

Dr. Hoag. Elsa caught a glimpse of him bending over a patient, the nurse beside him swiftly handing him gauze to cover a packed wound.

She had sped on halfway down the hall before she wheeled and sped back. The nurse was her mother. She wondered if either one saw the other as an individual or merely as a means of getting the torn body into intensive care.

Elsa had yet another shock. Reaching admittance, where she was to pick up a mauled baby from an hysterical mother, she found a man gently gathering information from the woman and writing it down. Salvorn, his light sports suit a gruesome sight, spotted with oil, with great splashes of blood.

He might be a multimillionaire with the future of Port Haven Hospital in his hands, but he was first a man with love of his fellow man. The playboy of his yesteryears had vanished or been vanquished.

She met Steffner once. He was hurrying to a new patient in Admittance from the surgery, where he had obviously just completed a difficult duty.

Elsa turned and sped for a fresh smock, handed it to him and heard him say, "Try to get some rest. The wind is abating. As soon as it dies and the waters subside, we'll be getting those trapped by the debris, the really possible terminals."

"But won't there be medical crews and nurses flown in when they can make a landing?"

"Meanwhile?"

But she wasn't tired. She found no one who was. Ruark, Bain, Mitzi, all of the guests who had been in her garden seemed as fresh as they had been that afternoon. Correction. Fresher, more eager for service.

"There is something to that second wind, isn't there?" she asked the nurse beside her.

"At a time like this, who thinks of oneself? Elsa, you were in the relaxer; did you see the Bain children? Bill phoned from your place to have them sent in." Elsa was aware it was Mitzi talking.

"They were there," she said, and flew off to a call of: "Hoyt. Lab."

There were thousands who spoke of that period as a nightmare. Not those at Port Haven Hospital. They had not time to think of what was going on outside the staunch walls of Port Haven Hospital, designed to stand in such a storm, north and east windows opened to offset a vacuum, south and west bulwarked.

Not until relief teams came in did they consider themselves. In the cafeteria, they looked from one to the other, determining where they could go now.

The great domes of the Salvorn mansion had finally given way. He'd

206

not risk his daughter there.

The yacht club had crumpled into the bay.

Dr. Hoag's apartment had shed its windows; his small cruiser had taken off for ports unknown.

Only the little tan cottage 'down the island' seemed to have survived without minor wreckage.

"So we'll sleep it off there," decided Dr. Hoag, then looked at Elsa's mother. "How many can we put up?"

Just the small group at the table was indicated. Elsa glanced at another table where Mitzi seemed to be acting as hostess to Bain, Ruark and a few others.

It was Mitzi who spoke for them. She came over, looked at each defiantly and said they were offering their resignations. They wanted no more of an island such as this.

Bob Latoret rose and smiled apologetically at Elsa. "That girl needs a test run. Mind?"

"You know what I wrote you."

Salvorn looked from one to another, then rubbed his hands. "Well now, that saves you from having to discharge the malcontents, eh, Hoag? After last night, they must see, as do I and perhaps — " He looked at Mrs. Hoyt. She nodded. "But we acknowledge and salute your farsightedness.

"Have any of you any realization how many patients were turned away from the other two hospitals because those edifices were not able to stand up to the storm? Wards had to be emptied, all south and west rooms vacated.

"A lesson we can learn: farsightedness in all things from government to personal life.

"And incidentally, Hoag, from reports I have, the repairs on the others more than offset your initial investment here. From now on we work as a team, right?"

"After he's had sufficient rest." Mrs. Hoyt spoke briskly. "He looks like the wrath. I hardly recognized him. Paul, suppose we take a run up to — oh, say Wyoming for a couple of weeks. Yes, Sam, that wind blew in my blocked door. I admit I was blind to his intrinsic value to the human of the species."

They went off two by two as though

Elsa were no more than a chair drawn up to the table. Then she saw Dr. Steffner looking at her, laughing.

"I planned it that way," he told her. "Hop into your mufti or a clean uniform; look at what you're wearing. I'll be waiting on the east side."

So he was going to drive her home? Well, that was something. Bob had fallen for Mitzi's wiles. Perhaps he could so charm her Mrs Bain could mend her marriage. But what of the Mitzis and the Ruarks? There were none better in their particular field. Why couldn't they accept that and not want, or need to dominate the whole?

Steffner drove Elsa back to the tan cottage by a roundabout way. Streets were so covered with litter, with halves of buildings, with roofs and with broken glass, he had to use discretion. He braked suddenly as a tall palm gave up life with a deep sigh and feel across the cleared space for which he was heading.

"Elsa, about yesterday: Hoag was worried about you, I more so. I was afraid I'd commit some grave error if you were there with that uncaring crowd.

I had to have you around. I want you around always."

"But I thought you hated me for letting Mitzi in, then moving along with her crowd."

"I knew your reason, and I had a guard set over you."

"A what?"

"Your Mrs. Misinformation. I once had occasion to realign a leg for her, and she gave me her devotion. She overheard a conference in that garden between your unwanted guest and a couple of men. She knew what they planned to do to you: a dose of pills to which you admitted you had an extreme allergy. Not dangerous; just devastating to your morale and poise. Then they would lay this at Hoag's door, a final *coup de grâce*, forcing Salvorn to foreclose."

"Doctor, does anyone ever win that way? I worried, stewed, felt I was intruding, but somehow I had to keep on. Then — well the storm took over. I truly believe there would have been something else if not the storm. Like the hospitals that were not prepared, neither could they have stood up to a marrow-searching blow."

"Let's give thanks for this crashed palm tree. Think what the natives might say if they found two of Port Haven Hospital's staff in a tangled embrace. Ah, Elsa, I've waited a long time for you."

THE END

Other titles in the
Ulverscroft Large Print Series:

TO FIGHT THE WILD
Rod Ansell and Rachel Percy

Lost in uncharted Australian bush, Rod Ansell survived by hunting and trapping wild animals, improvising shelter and using all the bushman's skills he knew.

COROMANDEL
Pat Barr

India in the 1830s is a hot, uncomfortable place, where the East India Company still rules. Amelia and her new husband find themselves caught up in the animosities which seethe between the old order and the new.

THE SMALL PARTY
Lillian Beckwith

A frightening journey to safety begins for Ruth and her small party as their island is caught up in the dangers of armed insurrection.

THE WILDERNESS WALK
Sheila Bishop

Stifling unpleasant memories of a misbegotten romance in Cleave with Lord Francis Aubrey, Lavinia goes on holiday there with her sister. The two women are thrust into a romantic intrigue involving none other than Lord Francis.

THE RELUCTANT GUEST
Rosalind Brett

Ann Calvert went to spend a month on a South African farm with Theo Borland and his sister. They both proved to be different from her first idea of them, and there was Storr Peterson — the most disturbing man she had ever met.

ONE ENCHANTED SUMMER
Anne Tedlock Brooks

A tale of mystery and romance and a girl who found both during one enchanted summer.

CLOUD OVER MALVERTON
Nancy Buckingham

Dulcie soon realises that something is seriously wrong at Malverton, and when violence strikes she is horrified to find herself under suspicion of murder.

AFTER THOUGHTS
Max Bygraves

The Cockney entertainer tells stories of his East End childhood, of his RAF days, and his post-war showbusiness successes and friendships with fellow comedians.

MOONLIGHT
AND MARCH ROSES
D. Y. Cameron

Lynn's search to trace a missing girl takes her to Spain, where she meets Clive Hendon. While untangling the situation, she untangles her emotions and decides on her own future.

NURSE ALICE IN LOVE
Theresa Charles

Accepting the post of nurse to little Fernie Sherrod, Alice Everton could not guess at the romance, suspense and danger which lay ahead at the Sherrod's isolated estate.

POIROT INVESTIGATES
Agatha Christie

Two things bind these eleven stories together — the brilliance and uncanny skill of the diminutive Belgian detective, and the stupidity of his Watson-like partner, Captain Hastings.

LET LOOSE THE TIGERS
Josephine Cox

Queenie promised to find the long-lost son of the frail, elderly murderess, Hannah Jason. But her enquiries threatened to unlock the cage where crucial secrets had long been held captive.

THE TWILIGHT MAN
Frank Gruber

Jim Rand lives alone in the California desert awaiting death. Into his hermit existence comes a teenage girl who blows both his past and his brief future wide open.

DOG IN THE DARK
Gerald Hammond

Jim Cunningham breeds and trains gun dogs, and his antagonism towards the devotees of show spaniels earns him many enemies. So when one of them is found murdered, the police are on his doorstep within hours.

THE RED KNIGHT
Geoffrey Moxon

When he finds himself a pawn on the chessboard of international espionage with his family in constant danger, Guy Trent becomes embroiled in moves and countermoves which may mean life or death for Western scientists.

TIGER TIGER
Frank Ryan

A young man involved in drugs is found murdered. This is the first event which will draw Detective Inspector Sandy Woodings into a whirlpool of murder and deceit.

CAROLINE MINUSCULE
Andrew Taylor

Caroline Minuscule, a medieval script, is the first clue to the whereabouts of a cache of diamonds. The search becomes a deadly kind of fairy story in which several murders have an other-worldly quality.

LONG CHAIN OF DEATH
Sarah Wolf

During the Second World War four American teenagers from the same town join the Army together. Forty-two years later, the son of one of the soldiers realises that someone is systematically wiping out the families of the four men.

THE LISTERDALE MYSTERY
Agatha Christie

Twelve short stories ranging from the light-hearted to the macabre, diverse mysteries ingeniously and plausibly contrived and convincingly unravelled.

TO BE LOVED
Lynne Collins

Andrew married the woman he had always loved despite the knowledge that Sarah married him for reasons of her own. So much heartache could have been avoided if only he had known how vital it was to be loved.

ACCUSED NURSE
Jane Converse

Paula found herself accused of a crime which could cost her her job, her nurse's reputation, and even the man she loved, unless the truth came to light.